PRAIRIE BLOSSOMS

KIM SMART

Prairie Blossoms is dedicated to all those who have suffered trauma. May you create a life filled with love. It is with immense gratitude that I also dedicate this book to those special friends and family who have shared their deeply personal journey from painful places through healing. Your light is ever-important in this life filled with shadows.

1

———

$\mathcal{L}$oretta glanced around the Davies' large living room, full of Christmas cheer, family fun, and familiarity. The Davies were her daughter Pauline's in-laws, and Loretta felt blessed to be included as part of the family. She spotted Dan and Yvette together and headed their way.

"Yvette, Dan, it has truly been a fabulous day!" Loretta smiled gratefully. "I'm going to head out before it gets too late. I see the wind is coming up and my car isn't very heavy for these roads, which is why I don't venture out in the winter much."

"Always a pleasure to have you here with us, Loretta," Yvette said fondly. "I'm sure we'll see more of each other, with our new grandbaby coming."

Dan nodded in agreement. "I'll see you out and check on the road conditions out there."

Loretta made the rounds, embracing everyone with a last Merry Christmas hug. The atmosphere was festive, the air filled with the joy of sharing and special announcements. She paused at her daughter Pauline and son-in-law Chance. "You two are going to make me a grandma! I'm so happy and so proud of both of you."

She reached up and tucked a strand of hair behind Pauline's ear. "I can't believe you kept it a secret from me, but then you're so busy I haven't seen much of you. Maybe this will make you slow down and take care of yourself."

"Oh, Mom. You worry too much. Chance and I are taking good care of each other and our little peanut, right honey?"

"Yes ma'am, we are. I'm sorry we waited so long to tell you, but we really wanted to share with the whole family at the same time. We are more excited than you can imagine, and I promise - Pauline can spend as much time as she wants with our little one. She doesn't need to go back to work ever, if she doesn't want to."

"You're a great man, Chance. Thank you for loving my girl so much."

Chance put his arm around Pauline and pulled her close. "Truly my pleasure Loretta. Hey, is your phone charged up? If you have any trouble at all, give me a call and I'll be right there to give you a hand."

"I'll call if I need to." Loretta, a slight, Sioux woman turned to find Brian, Chance's uncle who came from New Clay Mound township near the White River. She held her petite hand out. "It was sure nice to meet you, Brian. You've got some traveling to do to get home, too, unless you're bunking here."

"Yeah, I just checked with one of my boys who lives near me. He said there was some talk of closing the highway earlier, but the wind has died down there. I'll need to get home and check on the cattle, though. Hate the thought of any of them being somewhere other than where they are supposed to be, ya know, 'specially in this weather."

"Well, you be safe."

"Me and my one-ton will be fine, so long as the snow's not blowing too hard. These older eyes get lost amongst the snowflakes sometimes." Brian smiled at his own feebleness, a product of living a long, stubborn life on the rugged plains.

With hat down over her ears, scarf around her shoulder, winter gloves, long parka that nearly swallowed her, and Sorel winter boots laced up to mid-calf, Loretta walked to her car. Dan followed, shovel and broom in hand.

"You can surely stay here in a spare room if you want to, Loretta."

"You know Biggie wouldn't have had a problem taking these conditions on. Now that he's passed, I can't let the weather stop me, or I'll be sitting home crocheting baby blankets all the time. I'll take it easy. This grandma-to-be wants to stay alive for that new little one."

She started the car and turned on the defrost while Dan swept the car headlights, taillights and windows off.

"That sure is exciting news for us, isn't it? You and Yvette will have to fight over snuggling time. I can see it now, there will be a new snuggle calendar on the fridge."

They shared a laugh. "Okay, Dan. It looks great. Glad you have these yard lights here. I'll send Pauline a message when I get home. Should be about twenty minutes or so."

"Sounds good. Thanks for coming out, Grandma. We'll see you soon."

LORETTA GRIPPED the wheel of the Ford Escape and headed back to town, to the home she had shared first with Biggie before he passed away a couple of years ago, and then Pauline, before she married Chance. She missed Biggie at times like this. Nothing scared him. She had always been like a thrush - small, with a sweet voice and bright eyes, but aggressive if anyone threatened her family. That aggression, however, did not come through when she was the one threatened. Her childhood taught her that was not safe. Instead, she cowered and felt diminutive amongst the threats around her.

Tonight was no different. Snow was falling but hadn't accumulated much on the previously plowed roads. About half-way home, just before getting on the highway, the wind kicked up and she lost visibility. In a panic, she pressed the brakes harder than she knew she should. She heard snow scraping under the car and it stopped suddenly. Holding her breath, she turned on the windshield wipers to clear the piled snow. The headlights burned into a snowbank. She put the car in reverse. The wheels spun, but the car would not budge. She tried to open the door; a snowbank stopped the door from opening more than a few inches. Pulling the stocking cap down so it nearly covered her eyes, Loretta climbed all the way to the back of the car, opened the hatchback door and climbed out. Using the flashlight on her phone, she discovered that the two rear wheels were not fully settled on the ground and would not get traction.

Pauline was about the only person she ever called, so the number was easy to find on the phone. "Pauline, Pauline, can you hear me? Pauline?"

"Hi, Mom. Are you home already? Oh, no!" The chatter in the room faded so Pauline could hear. "We'll be right there. On this side of the highway, right?"

She whispered to the waiting crowd, "She landed in a snowbank." Pauline paused for confirmation. "Okay, Mom. Put your flashers on and climb back in to stay warm. If your tailpipe isn't buried it's fine to run your car and keep the heat on."

Chance rushed to get his jacket.

"Hey guys." Brian already stood at the door, coat and gloves on, with hat in hand. "No need for y'all to go out there. I'm headed that way. I've got everything I need to pull her out of a snowbank on that big rig of mine. I'll ring back if I need any help."

"Thanks, brother!" Dan said. "I'm sure she's just right there up by the corner with the highway. There's a spot there used as a cattle crossing and there's no wind break. I've seen it before. Heck, Yvette's been in that same situation more than once there."

"Ain't no secrets around here," Yvette grimaced. "It's true. I have been there over the years, probably some of our kids have, too."

Chance, Jesse, Steve, and Stella looked at each other, pointing fingers and laughing.

"Anyway, sure do appreciate it and you call back here if you need more help. Make sure that young lady gets home, won't ya?"

"Sure will. Not a problem." Brian said his final farewells and headed into the cold.

Loretta watched as headlights approached in the rear-view mirror. She turned the ignition off and climbed out the back hatch of the car to greet Chance, but was surprised to see his uncle Brian.

"Hey there, Loretta! I hear you got into a duel with a snowbank."

"I was overly optimistic, I guess."

"Ya. Your little Ford there is mighty, but maybe a little low to the ground. Bet them back tires just spin, don't they?"

"They look like they could almost get traction, but not quite."

"I'll give you a couple of options. I can shovel a bunch of snow under those tires and see if we can't try to push it out, but we really can't get ahold of the front end and push. Or if you're comfortable with the idea, I can put a tow strap on and just drag you backward onto the road. I guess there's a third option. We can just leave it 'til tomorrow and deal with it then. I could take you home or back up to the ranch, there."

"I trust you to just pull it out, Brian. Then I can get home tonight and let the kids know I'm safe."

"Sounds good. Why don't you hop up into the truck

there and stay warm. I'm just going to get 'er hooked up here and back up a bit."

LORETTA CRAWLED into the truck's cab, using the running boards to boost her petite body up. She moved the rancher's tools and extra leather gloves over to perch on the outside of the seat. The truck smelled like hay and oil. Biggie's work truck often smelled the same, when he was working as a ranch hand. He had been on her mind all day with thoughts of their last, painful Christmas together. The words, spoken when he handed her that last Christmas present, hung in the air. *Honey, I know our life has not been an easy one. I wanted the stars and the moon for you, but this old fart just couldn't get lift-off. We had fun. We laughed. We have a beautiful daughter, and I believe that neither of us doubted that we were loved. At least I hope that's true for you. I have this one last chance to give you something I always wanted for you. Rett, there's a gift in my sock drawer. I had Pauline put it there months ago. I don't have the strength to get it. Can you bring it out here and open it, please?*

In that box Loretta found the most beautiful diamond engagement ring. Tears fell as his words continued to flood her memories. *Finally, the diamond I always promised. Better late than..."*

Brian, a tall, sturdy man pulled the driver's door open and slid into his seat. "Okay, are you ready?"

Loretta, looking away and wiping tears from her face, responded, "Let's see what you can do."

"Alright then. Here we go." Brian expertly pulled the

car out of the snowbank and back onto the road in one smooth movement. "Let's go check for any front-end damage."

As they walked from the truck to Loretta's car, Brian asked, "Did you feel a hard hit when you landed in the snowbank?"

"No, I really didn't. Mostly what I heard was the crunching underneath and then there was a slow stop. The wind just blew that snow like crazy right then and I couldn't see." Loretta noticed that the wind had died down and the stars were dancing brilliantly in the dark night sky. "Would be kind of hard to prove now, with the calm air."

"Yeah, that's South Dakota for ya. Like they say, if you want the weather to change, just wait around for five minutes."

"Well, there's your license plate imprinted into the snowbank. Your car doesn't seem to have suffered any. Why don't you try to start it up and see how it does?" Brian opened the driver's door for Loretta. The car started right up.

"Ok. Here's what we're gonna do. You drive to your house, take as much time as you need, and I'm going to follow you. I'll stay back a bit so my headlights aren't blinding you in your rear-view mirror."

"Oh, really, I don't think there's…"

Brian held his hand up. "Please. It's the least I can do to make sure you get home and can tell the mother-to-be that you're home safe. I won't have it any other way so you might as well not argue with me. It's the right thing to do."

"Yessir, no arguing," Loretta responded quietly. "I'm probably going to be pretty slow until I get into town."

"Don't you worry none about this. I've been down this road before with my own family, and it's just no bother at all. Take all the time you need."

"That's kind of you. I'll get started now."

"Good. That's good. I'll see you in town."

LORETTA'S RIDE to town was uneventful. *Biggie Whyte, I bet you're having a great laugh over this one!* Her husband used to like to tease her about her driving. *Always so scared behind the wheel, you are. Give 'er a li'l more gas. She's not going to be a runaway like your ol' pony, Scout.* Loretta had told him about the painted pony she had when she was a young girl. A rattlesnake startled it and it took off with her bareback. Loretta had no idea how to control the horse and ended up getting thrown into a corral and breaking her arm.

BY THE TIME they pulled into the driveway, Loretta was more relaxed, and happy to be home. She immediately called Pauline to let her know she made it safely. And just as Brian got out of his truck, she responded to Pauline on the phone, "Uh, yeah, I guess it was like being rescued by a knight in shining armor. His truck is silver."

Brian kicked at an ice chunk in the driveway and quietly laughed.

"Ok Pauline, honey, I'm going to let you go now. You

guys be safe gettin' home. You've got precious cargo on board. Love you, too."

She turned to Brian and held her hand out. "Thanks so much for the rescue, Brian. I hope I haven't made you too late to get home safely yourself."

Returning the handshake, Brian responded, "Absolutely no problem, Loretta. I'm sure everyone's glad to know you are back home safe and sound. I'll be head…"

"Do you need a cup of coffee or something for the road?"

"Thanks, but no. I'll be fine. In fact, it's going to be a beautiful ride down through the Badlands tonight, with the sky as clear as it is now."

"Let's hope it stays that way. I didn't realize you got to your place through the National Park."

"That's right. I'll head south now and then veer off to the east after a bit. I'm just outside the park on the southeast side. Being that close to the Badlands is the best thing about my place actually. They've become like a part of me. Not sure you could separate us without me bleeding to death." He paused for a second. "Oops! Sorry. Now that I've said it, that sounds a bit morbid."

"That's okay. I do completely understand what you're saying. I wouldn't live anywhere else, myself."

"Alright then. I'm going to take off. It was great to get to know you a bit, Loretta, and congratulations again on that blooming grandbaby."

2

———

"Hey, old man! How's it going?" A stocky young-twenties blonde, with cowboy hat in hand, stepped into Brian's kitchen with a concerned look on his face.

"Hey there, Chad! Come on in. I'm just fixin' to have a fried egg sandwich." Brian flipped an egg in the pan on the stove. "Shall I break an egg for you?"

"Naw, I ate already."

"Well then, how 'bout a cup of coffee?"

"Sure. You're going to have to expand your morning menu Dad, or you're going to get bored."

"Bored? Heck, I'm already bored. After thirty-two years of waking up to morning prayer time with your mom, followed by a cup of the best coffee and breakfast a man could ever ask for, you bet I'm bored with a can of fruit cocktail and a fried egg sandwich. But I'm still eating and still moving forward with all four limbs, so I count my blessings where I can."

Chad frowned. "I know, you're a strong man, Dad.

Never a doubt about that, but it seems you're just not, well, you're not hanging out with us as much. You're always welcome to join us for dinner. Samantha makes enough to include you every night and sets a place at the table for you. For so long you joined us, and now you just don't show up."

"Sorry 'bout that. Tell Sam that I'll call when I'm coming; no need to have a plate for me otherwise."

"It's not so much that, Dad. It's that we miss you. Ever since you went to Uncle Dan's for Christmas it seems like you've had a lot on your mind and you're just not…so approachable."

"Is that so?" Brian popped the top on the can of fruit cocktail and slid it across the table toward his plate. "You sure I can't get you something besides coffee? Humor me. Have a piece of toast or a banana or something. You know I hate eating alone."

"Sure. I'll make a slice of toast. You have any peanut butter?"

Brian got the peanut butter out of the cupboard while Chad put bread in the toaster.

"So how is Sam? And her job? Kids giving her any trouble down there at the country school?"

"Sam's good, Dad. She loves teaching. She's young and relates really well to the kids. Sometimes she finds the parents more difficult. Generally, all goes well, but once in a while a student misses several days with no contact or doesn't do their homework and she can't get ahold of anyone at home. Usually, it turns out someone was sick in the household or there was a death in the family that took them away. You know some of the folks she deals with.

There's drinking and drugging involved for some. There are a couple of students she would love to bring home with her."

"Get her a bottle calf. That'll push off some of that nurturing angst until you kids are ready to have some of your own."

Chad let the comment settle. He felt tension in the way his father was talking, and it was unsettling. His speech was slow and he was distracted.

Brian broke the silence with business talk. "How's your calving going? You had some early deliveries, didn't ya?"

"It's been a little rough," Chad admitted, as he reached for his toast. "I lost a set of early twins in that storm last week. I couldn't find the mom. She was down in the breaks and I just couldn't get to her in time. She survived but I'll probably have to let her go. This is her second year to have preemies. It was probably a chance I shouldn't have taken, to keep her on, but lesson learned, I guess."

"Yeah, we all have those. I remember the second year your momma was sick…" Brian took a long swallow of coffee. He hadn't talked about Jerri Anne for quite a while with Chad, or anyone. "You were still away at school then, but the nights were terrible for her. Once the cancer spread to her liver and pancreas the pain was unbearable, especially at night. I had a cow that twisted her leg in a prairie dog hole, and she delivered early. I knew she was injured, but just couldn't juggle all the balls and get to her in time. I needed to be with your mother, seeing that she got morphine as often as she could just to give her enough of a fog to forget the pain for a few minutes at a time."

"I'm sorry you had to do that alone, Dad."

"No, don't do that. I chose to do it, and I wasn't alone. Your brother Ty was able come around and spot me some. Sissy came by and helped when she could. I think you, being the youngest, I wanted to protect you as much as I could from the hard parts. Yvette came and stayed with her a lot during that time, too. Your aunt Yvette, she's some kind of angel, you know."

"I do know. I bet she sent you home at Christmastime with a freezer full of food, too, didn't she?"

"Of course, she did. I've been picking at it some. I think she packaged up about thirty servings of that famous lasagna of hers. In fact, let me send some of those home with you guys. I'll never eat all that up."

"Thanks. Sam will be happy to put that in her planned meals rotation. She's an organized woman, that one. I'm lucky to have her in my life."

"Yes, you are. When you gonna marry that woman?"

"We will, one day. Once we put our plans on hold when Mom passed, it just seems hard to pick it up again. She's still got that dress hanging in the spare room closet. She used to go look at it about once a week, but she hasn't done that in some time. We're in a good space and I guess neither of us feels a need to go through the ceremony right now."

"I'll give you the money to run off to Vegas if you want. It's neither here nor there to me, but I know women usually like the fancy wedding, and that's fine."

"Sam thought she wanted a big wedding, but I don't

think it's as important to her now. I'm not sure how her folks would feel, though. They're pretty traditional, but I'll sure share the idea with her and see what she says."

"Like I say, I'm not trying to make waves or push an agenda here, just take off the pressure, if anyone's feeling any."

"I get it, Dad, and I appreciate the thoughts. I really was thinking about you though and wanted to see how you are doing. I know this time of year is hard, with Mom's birthday and your anniversary. We keep wondering if you're going to hop on a cruise one of these years and escape the heaviness of the season."

"I've never really considered it. And, you're right. There's lots of things to remember this time of year, some good and some bad, but I think I do best stayin' busy. Being right here with the livestock keeps me pretty focused." Brian silently acknowledged that he was walking around like a dark cloud hung over him. *This is a dark season. It's hard not to have my sweetheart with me. I get so lonely.*

"So, we're hosting Easter dinner this year. Ty and Sissy both said they would come. They might bring dates. It could be fun. We are hoping you'll join us."

"Time to think about Easter already? Seems Christmas just passed."

"Well, it's early this year, at the end of next month, but we wanted to be the ones to host since we weren't together for Christmas. Think you can join us?"

"Sure, sure. I'll be there. You want me to pick up a pie or something? I'm sure Caroline down there at the four-corners bar and bakery place can hook me up with something appropriate."

"That would be fantastic. You pick the flavor and I'll let Sam know you're bringing a dessert. Want me to write it on the calendar?" Chad looked over to the kitchen wall where a calendar had hung for as long as he could remember. The calendar there now was dated for last December.

"I didn't pick up a new calendar. Guess some part of me decided to break that tradition. I'll remember. Surely the pastor will be talking about Easter at church. I don't forget that it comes with a dinner."

"We'll be around to remind you."

"Say, before you take off this morning, think you could help me fix a little fence? I've got a weak spot over at the Turnow turn-off. Looks like a post rotted out at the bottom."

"Sure, happy to help."

____

3

The winter months passed, and mid-March came quickly. When Chance was unable to attend the month's ultrasound with Pauline, Loretta was more than happy to do so. They decided to add shopping and coffee time to the agenda for this special day.

Loretta held up a pale-yellow sleeper. "What about this little one, Pauline?"

"I don't know. It's okay, but kind of boring. I think I would rather go with a white one." Pauline was non-committal in choosing a coming home from the hospital outfit for their baby.

"Honey, what's going on?" Loretta had picked up on Pauline's unsettled feelings and lackluster mood. "You don't seem like yourself today."

"I'm sorry Mom. I don't know. Something just feels… off. It's kind of a feeling of doom hanging over me today."

"Is it because Chance couldn't come today? I'm sure he would have, if he could have."

"No…no, that's not it. And I want to thank you for coming with me. I know you had to go into work early so you could take the afternoon off. I do appreciate you, Mom."

Loretta wished Biggie was there. He would only have to slide his huge arm around Pauline's petite shoulders and pull her close and she would feel better. It always worked, for both of the women in Biggie's life. The winter months were especially hard without him. When he was still able, he managed the shoveling and car maintenance, kept the furnace running and saw that they got out at least once a week to be around others. *We have to get out and play, Rett, or we will not rise with the flowers in the spring.* That was Biggie. He lived by his own philosophies.

Loretta put her arm around Pauline. It didn't quite bring the same sense of safety and security as Biggie would have, but in this moment, she needed the physical touch as much as her daughter did.

"Are you worried about your doctor's appointment today? You've been feeling so good."

"Really, Mom…" Pauline wiped a tear from the corner of her eye. "I don't know what it is. Maybe it's just the hormones, but something seems off."

"Would you like to grab an afternoon treat instead of shopping? We've got about an hour before your appointment."

"That sounds good. There's a little bakery not far from the doctor's office. You probably remember - that one where we got those cranberry-orange scones when we were wedding shopping."

"I'm glad to hear that place is still open. Yes, sounds great."

———

"Mom, you don't talk much about Dad, and I can't tell if that's because you're trying to protect my heart, or yours. I sure do miss him and it's okay if you talk about him with me."

Loretta put the cup of tea down. "Oh, honey. I hope you know that I miss your dad terribly and I think about him all the time. I just didn't want to bring sadness to our every conversation anymore. There is something new and exciting to look forward to with the baby coming and we will be sharing stories of your dad with the baby soon. You know he would be so excited for you and Chance."

"I…we... do know that. We talk about how he would want to take the baby fishing as soon as he could and for rides in the old truck, and just sit and hold it for hours."

"I think Dan will want to, also, don't you? And of course, Yvette and I will fight over who gets to hold the baby every chance we can."

"That's for sure. This baby will not lack for love, but I do think about Dad and what he's missing."

"Mmhmm, me too. A lot."

———

After a long silence, Pauline checked her phone for the time. "I think we can meander over to the OB's office now. We'll still be a little early, but maybe they can get the ultrasound done."

"You still don't want to know the baby's sex, right? I mean, what if the tech just blurts it out?"

"They all know we don't want to know. It's a flag that comes up in the electronic record, I guess. But, if they slip, they slip, and we live with it."

"Good afternoon, Pauline. Come on back and we'll do your ultrasound. Is Grandma coming back too?"

"Of course! Come on, Mom. Let's get a peek at little peanut here."

"Let's just double check things here. Your due date is May 18, putting you at 31 weeks now." She pointed to the table for Pauline to climb up. "You know the drill. Go ahead and lie back and lift your shirt for me. Good, thanks. Grandma, if you could just stand right up by mom's head, you'll be able to see the screen, too. Yeah, there you go."

"Okay, first I'm going to take some measurements of baby's legs and then head, and we'll look at the organs. If I remember correctly, you want to be surprised at birth by the gender, right? So I'll skip those parts, or at least turn the screen away from you."

The ultrasound technician started the scan. "Looks like you have good fluid for the baby to live in. Right here, if baby will just hold still, I will quickly measure the femur."

"So that said 70 mm. Is that good?" Pauline was

watching every move the baby made and every number that showed up on the screen.

"Well, I can't give you any official interpretations of the data. The doctor has to do that, but 70 millimeters is on the upper end of normal for 31 weeks. Your husband is pretty tall, isn't he, if I remember right?"

"He is, and he has brothers who are even taller, so that's no surprise. You can't really tell by looking at me, but my dad was really tall, too. I take after Mom." Pauline looked at her mom and smiled. Pauline was not as petite as Loretta, but she was nowhere near as tall as Biggie was. She also seemed to have her mom's metabolism. She stayed thin. Even during pregnancy, she didn't have the full hips that a lot of women get. Her breasts were growing, but not as noticeably as others'. Pauline worried a lot.

"Okay, now I'm going to measure baby's abdominal circumference and something we call BPD, short for biparietal diameter." The technician moved the ultrasound wand around until she got a good view of the baby's belly.

"Are those the baby's kidneys?"

"Good eye. Yes, they are. Baby's belly looks good."

"Mom, look at baby's heart beat. Isn't that the coolest?"

Loretta couldn't speak. Joy silenced her voice and created tears in her eyes. She nodded.

The ultrasound tech quickly looked around the baby's head, turned the screen toward her and excused herself from the room. "I'm going to go see if Dr. Knox is ready to see you. Just stay put for now." She moved swiftly out of the room without saying more.

Pauline felt panic rise within. "That's really weird, Mom. The doctor never sees me in here and she turned the screen away. I knew something was wrong. I just knew it."

Loretta placed a hand on Pauline's cheek and looked her in the eye. "Take a deep breath and say a prayer, honey. Let's just let the doctor come in and talk, okay? You've been feeling well and you saw that baby's heart beat. It was strong, right?"

"Yeah, it was, but I'm scared."

<hr>

AFTER ABOUT AN ETERNITY, which in reality was only five minutes, Dr. Knox and the technician, Susan, walked back into the room. "Hi Pauline. It's good to see you again."

Dr. Knox slid onto the stool behind the ultrasound screen but didn't take her eyes off Pauline's. "How are you feeling? You're looking good."

"I'm good. Just feel pregnant, you know."

"Yeah, that happens about now for a lot of women. Susan asked me to come in and take a look at baby. Your measurements are looking right on target, baby's heart is strong, but there was a little spot in the brain that we are curious about. Let me just take a look here." Dr. Knox took a quick look through the ultrasound and then turned the screen so Pauline and Loretta could see it with her.

"Again, everything looks good. Baby is measuring

right on schedule. Maybe a tall baby. I looked at the baby's parts and all look good there, too, but I'll keep the baby's gender secret. What I do want to show you is something in the baby's brain. Now, I'm going to tell you that what I see is nothing to worry about, and you're going to worry anyway, because that's what moms do. Please, try to keep yourself from fretting about this. It happens in two percent of all pregnancies and resolves itself over time."

Dr. Knox pointed to a dark spot on the screen. "See this dark spot, almost a circle, inside this white area here? This is what we call a choroid plexus cyst. This is the area that makes spinal fluid that flows in tubes to the brain. Sometimes those tubes get stuck together and fluid builds up between them, so it creates this spot that looks like a cyst. Now, sometimes this condition is part of a chromosomal condition known as Trisomy 18, but in your case, your screening test was negative and there are no other indicators with baby's heart or limbs, stomach or face that are consistent with Trisomy 18. So, I think we can expect the cyst to resolve itself over time. Usually, they resolve by about 28 weeks, but I have seen them as late as 36 weeks. I think if we do another ultrasound in two weeks, we will see that cyst getting smaller or it may be gone completely."

"Does it keep the baby's brain from growing or developing?"

"No. There is no reason to believe that the baby's brain is not growing normally. And, good news is that baby has already turned head down. If it stays that way, there's no reason to be concerned about a breech birth.

Your weight gain is good. You may not have the 40 extra pounds a lot of women have after delivery, but you are obviously providing enough for the little one to grow normally in the uterus."

Dr. Knox paused and looked to Pauline and Loretta. "Do you have any other questions for me?"

Pauline looked to Loretta, then to Dr. Knox. "What should I tell Chance?"

"Just what I told you, and I'll ask the nurse to print you out an explanation. This is not an unusual condition for us to see. It usually resolves itself without us needing to provide any intervention and you don't need to change anything that you are doing. You didn't cause this. We will do another ultrasound in two weeks. Until then, I'm advising you not to give it any energy. Just put it out of your mind." Dr. Knox paused again. "Does that make sense?"

"Hard to put it out of my mind," Pauline admitted. "But yes, thank you. I understand."

4

———

$\mathcal{P}$auline's hand shook as she put the key in the ignition. "See, I told you I had a bad feeling. I just knew something was wrong. This dark cloud just follows me everywhere."

"Pauline. Let's just pause a minute. What I heard Dr. Knox say is that this is nothing and will resolve without having anything bad happen to baby. In two weeks, you can have another ultrasound and it will be cleared or clearing, with nothing bad happening to the baby."

"Yeah, it's just this nagging feeling. I can't shake it."

Loretta calmly folded her hands and bowed her head. "Lord, I ask that you continue to protect Chance and Pauline's growing baby, and that you bring calm to Pauline in this time of testing for her. Bring your healing hand and allow baby Davies to continue the miraculous journey to birth and beyond. Bring peace to this family. I pray in Jesus' name. Amen."

"Amen." Pauline whispered and wiped away her tears.

"I don't know when you became such a prayer warrior, Mom, but thank you."

"Prayer has kept me sane since your daddy got sick. You remember I went to boarding school as a kid and learned to pray there. I may have rebelled for a long time after that, but I find great comfort in prayer now."

"You don't talk much about growing up, Mom. I don't even know my family from the reservation."

"Honey, when your daddy married me, I promised myself I would never look back at that life. It was a very rough life, and I wouldn't want it for you. My grandparents and parents are long dead and my half, step, and maybe, siblings are lost to me."

"Aren't you even curious about how your relatives are doing?"

"Of course, and I pray for their health and safety, but after this many years, it would be hard for me to find them, if they are even still living. I know it doesn't make sense to you because you had parents that loved you dearly and you married into a big happy family, but not all families are like that and there are things in my past that I just will not talk about for my own mental health. Some people are really toxic, and I found, for me, I needed to stay away from that, and I think it made a better life for both of us."

"I just can't help but wonder if there isn't something seriously wrong with the baby, and if so, if it's happened in the family at all before."

"That is a fair question. First, I trust your doctor to be on the level with you, and I believe that when you come back in two weeks there will be resolution of the cyst."

"You're probably right."

"Second, I promise you I'll give some thought to checking on my relatives. Maybe it's time I set aside my own fears and hurts. It's a very dark hole for me to go peering in."

"Okay, Mom. I won't ask anymore, but I do appreciate you thinking about it…for me…for the baby."

As they approached Buffalo Ridge, the two returned to the discussion about sharing the day's news with Chance. Tentatively, Loretta asked, "Honey, do you know what you're going to say to Chance? Do you want me to be there with you?"

"I don't even want to tell him, Mom. He'll just worry, and I don't want that for him."

"But honey, you can't keep it from him. He'll know you're worried."

"You're right. I have thought about it. I am going to give him the facts, and I have the information sheet the doctor gave me. I'll share that with him. I think I'm fine to do it alone. We will need some time together to just talk about what it could and could not mean. I'm sure he will want to go to the next appointment with me."

"I hope he can make it. I'm happy to be a back-up if you need. Thanks for letting me go with you today."

"I'm so grateful you were there, Mom. You were amazingly calm, and I really appreciate you."

"Hey, Loretta."

Loretta looked up quickly, startled out of her thoughts. She hadn't heard the customer come into the store where she worked in the afternoons, after cleaning motel rooms in the morning. It was a slow time of year for the store, and often hours passed without seeing a customer, until the children got out of school and stopped by for snacks. "Uh, oh, hi, Nancy."

"Where were you? Seems your thoughts were a million miles away."

"They were many miles away," Loretta admitted. "How can I help you today?"

"Actually, I was wondering if I could help you. Some of us ladies have been talking about making a quilt for Chance and Pauline's baby. We wondered if you had any of your own baby clothes, or something special that Biggie wore, that we could incorporate into the quilt."

Loretta pressed both hands into the counter to steady herself and responded in a shaky voice. "That's very nice of you. Can I…uh, think about it and get back to you? I'm sure there is something, but I, uh, yeah, I'll get back to you."

"Sure, that would be great. And if there's nothing, no sweat. We can certainly come up with fabric from our stashes, but we always try to bring something into the design from the family, if we can."

"That's sweet, and appreciated, I'm sure." Loretta's voice returned to its normal confidence. With relief, she quickly changed the conversation to local news.

THAT EVENING, Loretta slowly set the car keys on the kitchen counter and hung up her coat. She started the evening coffee pot, a habit started decades before with Biggie. Often, the still-full pot was emptied into the kitchen sink as she went to bed, but she couldn't stop herself from pushing that start button. She opened the door to the basement, flipped on the light and slowly made her way to the storage room. She pulled a large tote from where it rested on a shelf in the far back corner. With delicate shaking hands, she reached to the bottom of that tote and pulled out an old cigar box. A ragged hinge kept the cardboard lid attached. Gently setting it on the floor, she then closed the tote and pushed it back into the corner. Loretta found the old stepstool and climbed up to reach a smaller plastic tote, hugging it to her chest as she stepped back down. She lifted the lid and looked at the items inside. She gently picked up the old cigar box and carried both back to the kitchen, where she set them on the table and poured herself a cup of coffee. *Oh, Biggie, I could really use your company now,* she thought as the clock chimed, announcing the six o'clock hour.

Loretta took a long swallow of hot coffee, as if to torture her esophagus with the hot liquid. She first opened the plastic tote. One-by-one she removed the items and looked at them. A tiny yellow floral print dress, with matching bloomers, made by an elderly friend. White booties and jacket knit by another. Seven outfits, a receiving blanket, and crocheted throw, all made for Pauline. Biggie's mother was elderly and nearly blind when she crocheted the throw, specially made for Pauline's baptism.

Loretta remembered the day Pauline was born. Biggie was so proud of his baby girl. He stared at her through the nursery window for hours, bringing Loretta in the wheelchair when she was able. Loretta remembered being terribly nervous during the entire pregnancy, and scared of the required checkups with the doctor. She had held back her screams during delivery, biting her lips so hard that the nurses packed them in ice to stop the bleeding after the baby was born.

Fingering the tiny clothes, Loretta knew there was nothing that she would want the sewing ladies to cut up for a quilt. She would give them all to Pauline and Chance. If they had a boy, he could wear the white jacket and booties and use the throw and receiving blanket. Everything else could be saved for another pregnancy, if there would be another one. Loretta was grateful to have lived through her pregnancy with Pauline.

She stacked the clothes back into the tote and closed the lid. She would hand wash them later and, after they were dried and pressed, give them to Pauline. She finished the cup of coffee and refilled it before opening the cigar box.

Images of herself as a scared fourteen-year-old came to life, clutching that box as she quietly moved her tiny body on bare feet through the halls of the boarding school, down the dark stairs and up through a broken window in the basement. Her heart raced as her body remembered the fear. Fear of getting caught. Fear of the punishment that would follow. Fear of finding her way home to her parents. Fear of what she would do when she told them her secret. A secret she could no longer hide.

Loretta remembered running until she could run no more. She had only vague directions to her classmate's house but believed she could find it. The boarding school was in a small community in eastern South Dakota. A few white students, children of local families, went to school there, along with the American Indian children who had been brought there from all over the state, and beyond, to learn from the nuns and priests. As a class exercise, her classmate, Margaret had once drawn a map to the store her father owned. The family lived above the store, according to Margaret. Loretta drew on that memory and by dawn had found the building. She waited until there was a light on inside the home before walking up the stairs and timidly knocking on the door.

A pretty blonde woman, with a baby on her hip, answered the door. "Hello dear. Come in! Come in! You look white as a ghost."

Margaret's mother ushered Loretta into the kitchen and offered her a chair and a glass of water. She set the baby in a highchair and gave him a piece of toast. "I'm Mary. What's your name, honey?"

"Lo…Loretta, ma'am." Loretta had a different name before boarding school. She had a traditional name, given to her by her family, but she hadn't uttered it since she left home at the age of six. "I'm pleased to meet you."

"You don't look like you feel very well. Can I get you something to eat? Are you hungry? How about a piece of toast?"

"No, thank you ma'am. Can I just rest here a minute?" Loretta suddenly realized her plans were flawed. She would be sitting there when Margaret and the family's other children came to breakfast. "Um, actually, I should go."

She raced out the door and across the street, where she hid in a shrub-lined ditch, peering out periodically to see if the children's father had taken them to school yet. When she saw the kids pile into the car with Margaret's father and drive away, she went back up to see Mary. By then, she knew what she had to say to get Mary's help.

"My mother, she's very sick, and I need to get to her so I can see her before she dies. I haven't seen her since I was eight."

"How did you learn that she was sick, Loretta?"

"A relative stopped at the school and told me, but the nuns wouldn't let me go see her with him. They said they had no way to know if he was really a relative or if he was trying to kidnap me. They said it happened once and they didn't want it to happen to me."

"Have you tried calling your relatives to come get you?"

"I don't have any information to call them and the sisters won't let me call the hospital. I just need to get there. If... if you could loan me the bus money, I could get there and I promise I will pay you back."

Mary hesitated. "You know my children go to that school. I don't want to get in trouble with them."

"I won't tell anyone you helped me. I promise! I just have to get there. I have a terrible feeling that my mother doesn't have much time, and I will feel just awful if I don't get to see her and tell her how much I love her before she dies." Loretta hated lying. She knew it was a sin, but she believed the truth was a bigger sin.

"Let me just think. And here, you need to eat. You look like you're wasting away. There's a little bit of oatmeal left and here's a banana. You eat this while I change the baby and give this all a thought." Mary picked up the baby and left the room. Loretta picked at the food, listening to see if Mary was calling the school, or worse, the police.

Mary returned to the kitchen, hair tied up in a scarf, lipstick neatly coloring her lips, and a clean sweater on the baby. "I'm going to go down and meet my husband at the store when he gets back from taking the children to school. I will tell him the baby has an appointment. You watch out this window here, and when you see me put the baby in the car, you come on down, quietly, and crawl into the back seat with the baby. You can keep him company. It's a ways to the bus stop, as you may know."

"Oh, ma'am, I can't thank you enough! I really do appreciate you doing this, and I will pay you back. I'll be very quiet, and I will keep your baby happy."

THE OLDER LORETTA gently wiped the tears with her fingertips, as she experienced these memories of her younger self. She still felt remorse for lying to Mary, even though she had sent an envelope with $8.00 to repay the bus ticket. It took three years to get that money together, but she did it.

Loretta opened the cigar box. Inside lay patchwork squares she had gathered and sewn together in the dark while still at the boarding school. She had squirreled away the fabric squares, needle, and thread from the school's sewing room. She pricked her fingers hundreds of times while trying to piece a quilt together in those last days before running away. Those were frightening days, with the nuns scolding her for becoming pregnant and awaiting the arrival of the doctor to end the pregnancy. She was forbidden from talking about the pregnancy, or the man who forced her to become so. "You will burn in hell if you breathe one word of this to anyone, ever." The words were branded in her memory. It took over half her life and Biggie's support to gain perspective, start to forgive, and begin to heal from those events. And now, she was starting to pick at the fragile scab covering what happened next.

5

"Hey, Loretta. This is Brian - Brian Davies."

Loretta nearly dropped the phone. She never answered the phone when she didn't recognize the number, but this was the day that Pauline and Chance were at the doctor's office for a follow-up ultrasound. She was expecting to hear from them any minute.

"Uh, hi, Brian. This is Loretta. Oh, gosh," she sputtered. "You already knew that, sorry."

"Hi. I hope you don't mind; I got your number from Yvette. Did I get you at a bad time?"

"No. Actually, I was just expecting a call from Pauline, but it's okay. I'm sure she'll call later."

"Well, I won't keep you long. I just remembered when we were visiting at Christmastime that you mentioned you had a garage full of old tools and parts that your late husband had collected. I know this might sound strange, but I'm looking for a very specific old tool to fix a part on a very old tractor I have. I could try to describe it to you and maybe you know if there might be one around that I could buy from you."

"Um, we could try that. I'm at work right now, but I could look this evening when I get home."

"Well, the other thing is, I'm going to be 'round there later this week. Got to do some business in Rapid City. Maybe we could meet up and I could take a look myself? That might save you some trouble. I mean if you don't mind someone looking through the tools."

"Oh, no, I don't mind at all. It's fine. If you can use anything in there, you can certainly have it. Biggie would like to know that his precious tools are being put to use, if you know what I mean. It would be best if you took a look, since you know exactly what you need."

"Okay then. How 'bout Friday afternoon, say about 5:30? I'll be headed back home and that should be about the right time. It shouldn't take long."

"That would be fine. I'll be home from work then." Loretta's phone vibrated as she spoke. "Oh, say, Pauline's calling. We'll see you Friday. Good-bye."

"Goo…" Brian spoke to the dead phone line.

<hr>

"Hey, honey. Hi."

"Hi Mom, you're on speaker phone."

"Hi Loretta."

"Hey, Chance."

"You were right, Mom. There was nothing to worry about. Baby looks great."

"The cyst is gone?"

"It's about 60% smaller and on its way to being gone."

"That's fantastic news!"

"Yes, and everything else looks great, too," Chance announced. "Now your daughter can relax, I hope."

"Do you think so, Pauline? Can you relax?"

"Well, I don't know. Dr. Knox reminded me today that baby's due in less than two months and I suddenly thought of all the things that we need to do."

Loretta chuckled softly. "Babies have been born for centuries, even before there was a gift registry or baby shower. All that baby needs is love, a diaper change, and something to eat. No need to stress yourself out over the things the media says you need."

"Well, a name would be nice. Did you know you can't leave the hospital now until your baby has been given a name?"

"No, I didn't know that, but when you meet your baby, you will know what the name should be. They won't hold you hostage. You'll be ready."

"That's what I keep telling her. Either it's Brutus or Dolly."

"Oh, Chance! No wonder she's so worried. I would protest, too."

The three shared a laugh, relief from two long weeks of holding their breath and praying for this good outcome.

"You guys stay safe going home. Pauline, I have a couple things for you at the house when you have a minute to stop by. I'll leave them on the kitchen table."

"Okay, I'll probably be by tomorrow sometime. Is it okay to go in if you're..."

"You know it is, honey. It's fine."

Loretta did not give anything to the quilt ladies. She had already donated Biggie's clothes, at least the ones that were salvageable, to the Rescue Mission. The little baby quilt lay in the cigar box, in a drawer by her bed; she wasn't ready to part with it. She gave considerable thought to the conversation with Pauline, and all the memories and feelings that it stirred up. The issues were more than she could handle alone, so she made an appointment with a counselor in the city, to explore options, including just letting bygones be bygones. There was a nagging feeling that she needed to deal with the events that followed her departure from the boarding school.

Loretta was startled by loud rapping on her door. It was Friday evening, after a long workweek, and she had just put a cheap cardboard-tasting pizza in the oven. She didn't have much of an appetite, but knew she needed to eat something. After a few bites, the rest of the pizza would go in the fridge for lunches next week. As soon as she saw Brian standing on the porch, Loretta remembered that he was planning to stop by.

"Hey Loretta!" his friendly voice greeted. "How are you doing? Is this still a good time?"

"Ya…yes, this is a fine time," she stammered. She brushed the long salt-and-pepper hair away from her face, tucking the front strands behind her ears. She wished she had a mirror to make sure she didn't have smudges from work on her face. "I haven't been out to the garage to turn on the lights or anything. Do you want a coffee or water or something before you look out there for that tool you need?"

"Oh, no. I'm good, thanks. I'm sure I can find the lights if you don't want to…"

"No, no, it's fine. Let me just put some shoes on and I'll join you." Loretta slipped off the comfy old slippers and slid her feet into the sneakers sitting by the door.

"Nobody's been through this stuff," Loretta said as she opened the side door to the garage and flipped the light switch. "Except maybe Chance, looking for some tools."

Brian gazed around in amazement. "Wow! Who knew Biggie was such an organized fella? I didn't know him well, and I know he was a good worker out at Dan and Yvette's when he helped them out. But this place is like a museum!"

"Right. He was a little obsessive-compulsive."

"A little?" Brian's asked.

"Okay, maybe a lot. It was good for me. I didn't have to clean up after him, and he doted on me like crazy. It seemed he found value in almost every tool and scrap of metal anyone discarded in his direction. If you can make sense of his organizational ideas here, you're better than I am."

Brian looked around the garage, with pegboard-lined walls and shelves lined with toolboxes and cardboard boxes. "Well, it seems to me the tractor parts are divided by make and model, and then by year. The one I'm looking for should be…"

Brian walked to the northeast corner of the building and studied the shelves. "Right here." He pulled down a box and peered inside, before reaching in. He held out an old tool. "Well, I'll be darned. Unbelievable. Here it is."

"That is amazing! I can't believe it didn't take hours and hours to find that one thing. There's no way I would have found that, I don't care if you had drawn me pictures to scale. It wouldn't have happened." Loretta suddenly remembered the pizza in the oven. "Oh, I can't believe it. I forgot I have a pizza in the oven. I'll be right back to…"

"I'll get the lights and close the garage back up," Brian called out to Loretta's back as she rushed to the house. He stood for a moment and gazed admirably at the organized collection in the garage before locking up and making his way back to the house. The porch door was open, with the odor of burnt cardboard drifting out. Loretta stood just inside the door, waving the last bit of smoke out with a dishcloth.

"Well, I would offer you a piece of pizza, but…" she laughed. "Maybe another time?"

"Oh, Loretta, I feel awful."

"Why? You didn't do anything. I'm the one with the swiss cheese memory."

"Would you let me buy you dinner, uh, for the tool and, uh, for distracting you from your cooking?"

"That's a nice offer, but it's not necessary, Brian."

"We both need to eat. Did you get your oven turned off? Let's just run downtown to the Buffalo Ridge Bar. I hear they have a good burger."

Loretta paused for a moment. She was hungry. "That does sound good. Sure. We can walk from here, it's just a couple of blocks."

"Great. Let me just put this tool in the truck. Maybe I could use your washroom before we head out?"

"Of course. Come on in, but don't mind the smoke in the kitchen." Loretta waved her hands through the slightly tainted air as they passed through the kitchen.

"Ah, it's not so bad in here. I can barely tell there was a fire." Brian laughed, trying to get Loretta to lighten up. He sensed her embarrassment for burning dinner.

Loretta laughed with him. "Oh, you come with jokes, do you? What a relief. I was afraid this would be a boring dinner."

"We shall see. Just let me wash up and then we can head downtown."

LORETTA TOOK the opportunity to brush her hair and put on a little blush powder and lip tint. She wasn't big into makeup, but had found in the past year that she felt better with a little color on her face.

THE TWO ENJOYED a casual dinner amongst a crowd of locals at the bar. They were interrupted several times by people who knew Loretta, and some who also knew Brian.

"Hey ol' man, good to see ya!"

Brian stood to shake hands with an old family friend, a big rancher in the area. "Well, I'll be! Timmers, how the heck are you? It's been a long time. You know Loretta Whyte?"

"Sure do. Ma'am, it's nice to see you again."

"You too." Loretta smiled but did not offer her hand. Wyatt Timmers was not one of her favorite locals. In their younger days, in a drunken fog, he had made some condescending comments about her American Indian heritage. Biggie landed a hard punch on his mouth, and he never did it again; but for Loretta, there was still an old pain when she saw Wyatt.

"Well, good to see you both. Wife's out in the truck. Better not keep her waiting any longer."

"That's right! Tell Marla hello for me," Brian called to Wyatt as he walked away.

THE EVENING PASSED QUICKLY, and before they knew it, they were again standing at Loretta's porch door.

"Loretta, I know it wasn't in your plans to burn a pizza and have to have dinner with a grumpy old rancher, but I'm sure glad it happened. It was great to see you again, and I haven't laughed so much for a long time."

"Thank you for dinner, Brian. I really did enjoy it. I had no idea such wit ran in the Davies' family."

"It doesn't. I got it all."

They laughed. Brian reached out for Loretta's hand as she turned to open the door. "I'm going to hit the road to home, but Loretta, I sure would like to see you again."

Loretta shifted her feet and looked to the ground.

"You don't have to answer me now, but would it be okay if I gave you a call sometime?"

Loretta bit her bottom lip and slowly nodded her head. "Uh-huh. Yes, I would like that. I truly did enjoy this evening."

"Okay, then." Brian squeezed her hand gently before dropping it and backing down the porch steps toward his pickup. "I'll be in touch. You take good care."

"You as well. Drive safely."

LORETTA FRETTED until the early morning hours, flipping through tv channels, wondering if Brian got home safely. Neither of them drank anything but water at dinner, so she wasn't worried about him drinking and driving, but at their ages, a heavy meal could bring on sleep easily. After a series of silent prayers, she finally fell asleep in her recliner. Sleep brought on a pleasant dream about nothing she could recall, but she felt happy.

6

———————

*L*oretta had waited two weeks for her first counseling appointment. By that time, she was full of uncertainty. "I'm just not sure that I want to dredge up all these memories and relive those things. I'm not convinced that the benefits outweigh the pain for me."

The counsellor understood immediately. "For right now, let's just explore what those benefits might look like for you."

"The whole idea of trying to track down any living relatives is to learn about our family health history. I guess I have almost thought of myself as being adopted since I was never really raised by my birth family, at least not for long."

"So, one benefit would be finding out if you have any living relatives, and another would be learning about any health problems they have had. Are there other benefits?"

"I have always thought about it, and when Biggie, my

husband, was alive, he encouraged me to do it if I wanted to, but I never did."

"Do what, Loretta?"

"Find out how she was."

"Who is 'she', Loretta?"

"The daughter I gave up for adoption when I was fourteen, after being raped by a man at the boarding school," Loretta blurted out the words before they could be pushed back down into that secret space inside.

"There's a lot wrapped up in that potential benefit Loretta, and I can understand your hesitation. You previously told me that you had counseling to address the circumstances at the boarding school and have come to a place of forgiveness in your heart for those events. Can you say more about the benefit to you, personally, for learning about how the daughter you adopted out is doing?"

"It would only be a benefit if she was thriving. I have a huge fear that somehow, my experiences early in life would have negatively impacted her. If, instead, she was adopted by a good family and had a good life, there would be so much relief for me. If she was healthy, that would also be a huge relief."

OVER THE NEXT TWO WEEKS, Loretta explored the feelings around finding her first daughter. Ultimately, she decided to contact the adoption agency. She also felt a need to continue therapy to nurture her well-being with the process.

"Loretta, when we last met, you were planning to contact the tribal adoption agency to see if you could learn about your daughter. Did you pursue that?"

"I did, and it seems I was wrong. When I went back to the reservation after I ran away from the boarding school, things weren't very good for me. My father had left my mother. She told me he was dead, but I don't know if that was true or not. She had another man living with her, and when I got there, they were having a big party. She took one look at me, called me names, and slammed the door in my face."

"Did you ever see your mother again, or have any resolution with her?"

"No."

"I can't imagine how that experience was for you. Where did you go then?"

"I went to my grandmother's house."

"In the same community?"

"Yes. I walked there. My grandmother took me in until I had the baby. I remembered that near my time for delivery we went into Rapid City to a catholic agency and talked to them about finding adoptive parents for my baby. The baby's dad was not native and my grandmother made a strong case for them to help out. She was skeptical about the baby having its best life if she was adopted by a family anywhere near my mother."

"So, your baby was adopted through Catholic Charities?"

"That's right. I have contacted them and they do have a way to contact my daughter. I have left my information with them, and they will share it with her if she is willing to meet me. They didn't share anything about her except that she was adopted out to a family in the Black Hills."

"You have done a very brave thing, Loretta. I know you had a lot of doubts about reaching out with uncertainty about the outcome."

"It's for my daughter Pauline and my future grandchildren, as much as it is for me."

"Well, I think it's brave and hope you recognize within yourself the strength it took to get here."

"Thank you. I think it's dawning on me, the inner strength I have. I leaned on Biggie a lot. He was my protector in many ways, and he propped me up a lot. In learning to live without him, I am learning a lot about myself and praying a lot for strength to face life as it comes up."

"That's an amazing insight, Loretta."

LORETTA LEFT COUNSELING feeling emotionally exhausted but with a sense of healing, and readiness to take additional steps to give herself good care. On the way home, she stopped at a chic boutique in Rapid City and bought a new pair of jeans and two tops, to celebrate spring and her personal gains. While driving back to Buffalo Ridge, the phone rang through her car. Knowing that baby Davies was due to arrive in the weeks coming up, she instinctively answered it without checking the caller ID. "Hi there. Loretta here."

"Hi, Loretta." She recognized Brian's voice immediately. "It's Brian...Davies."

"Hello, Brian. How are you?"

"Good. I'm doing good." After an awkward pause, or delay in the transmission, he continued, "And how are you?"

"I'm actually doing really well, thank you."

"That's great to hear. Say, I was just wondering, uh, if you would be interested in coming to our little community, New Clay Mound, next weekend. There's an Indigenous Day celebration. Ya know, I live right on the border of the reservation and our few merchants here like to pay special tribute to the Native Americans who do business here in town, with the sale barn, the grocery and such."

"Ummmm…I've never heard of this celebration before, but then I'm not really connected to the reservation. I left there a long time ago and never looked back." Loretta's thoughts drifted, and she felt her stomach turning into knots. "I appreciate the offer, Brian, but if I have to decide right now, I think I have to say no."

"Oh, no, there's no need to decide right now. I'd be happy to come up and get you. I just thought it might be a fun time for you to come down and see what's goin' on down here."

"That's kind of you, and I would like to see where you come from, but I'm just not sure this is the right thing for me right now." Loretta sensed that she could share with Brian the turmoil she felt about the reservation and her source of discomfort, but now was not the time or place to share it all. She did, however, feel compelled to provide some explanation. "I left the reservation when I went to boarding school very young, and really lost my ties to the area back then. Then Biggie and I married and really never went back there."

"Hey, that's fine. I'm open for whenever it feels right, and we can get the time off together. I know your busy season is coming up with the grandbaby coming and tourist season and all." Brian's voice became quieter and less enthusiastic.

Loretta felt bad. "Listen. Just because this isn't the right thing for us to do, I'm sure we can figure something out. We could meet half-way, or I could come all the way down there. I can make arrangements to adjust my day off if we need to."

"Sure. That'll work. I've got to work cattle and there will eventually be branding, but of course, I can get one of the boys to spot me some day."

"Hey Brian, I have an idea. If it wouldn't be too boring for you, let's meet up down in the Badlands, do a little sightseeing and grab some lunch at the resort down there."

"I really like that idea, Loretta. We could do it before it gets too busy with tourists. With that grandbaby due soon, I'll look to you to set the date. You want to just get back to me and let me know?" Brian's voice was livelier and more engaged.

"Let's shoot for the first Saturday in May, unless you have branding or something planned for then."

"Good news is that I'll have already branded by then and haven't offered to help anyone else yet for that time. We can talk about details later if you don't mind me calling on you again."

"Feel free to give me a call. I'll answer if I'm not at

work, and even then, if I'm on a break or not busy, I will answer. I sure do appreciate you thinking of me, Brian, and look forward to spending some time together. Seems I have so many friends who have left the area for one reason or another. It's good to know I've got another friend to do things with."

"Same here, Loretta. Thank you for being willin' to do something with this old man. Looking forward to it. I'll be in touch."

Brian wanted to continue to chat but didn't want to wear out his welcome. His initial uncertainties about making the call dissipated and he hung up wearing a smile.

7

———

"This is absolutely stunning, and to think it's practically in my back yard." Loretta stood, mouth agape as colors rose in the sky with the awakening of the sun.

"Sunrise in the Badlands inspires poets to write, musicians to compose and painters to paint. It's not like sunrise anywhere else in the world."

Brian had watched sunrises in many parts of the world, yet still found the greatest joy watching the vast sky fill with color while light rays illuminated the striations of the clay mounds below. He had suggested an early morning date for the sole purpose of sharing the sunrise. He picked Loretta up at 4:30 a.m. and asked her to have a thermos of coffee ready for them to share. He had baked banana muffins and brought them along. They were greeted at the Badlands National Park entrance by several resident bison and two enormous, big horn sheep rams standing guard over the sacred grounds. Brian drove to Sheep Mountain Table, parked, and suggested a mound to sit on while watching the sun appear on the horizon. Grey dawn surrendered to crimson, purple, and buff colored sky as the sun made her grand entrance. High clouds provided texture and dimension, reflecting pink and orange hues back to the sun. In a matter of twenty minutes, the light show was over and the sky became a brilliant blue, with silvery clouds hanging high.

"It is so quiet, so peaceful here." Loretta broke the long silence. Both were mesmerized by the light show and like coming out of a dream, she realized she was transported to a new place within herself.

"It is, indeed. But check it out. As we sit here, there's movement on the baked clay and in the grasses. Already the birds are lookin' for seeds and bits of grass are moving 'round."

"You're right, and the prairie dogs are moving too. I suppose if we look long enough, we could see rattle snakes coming out to sun themselves."

"Yep, that's true, sure could. Now this trail is a long one, 'bout fourteen miles I think, but we don't need to go that far."

"How about we just play it by ear. My only concern is that it's going to get hot out here by noon."

"Okay. Sounds good. I've got us some waters and some snacks in a backpack. Let me just grab that from the truck and I'll be ready."

"Do you want to polish off this coffee with me first? I wouldn't mind just taking in this view a few minutes longer."

After finishing the thermos of coffee, the two headed out on the Sheep Mountain Table trail. They hiked on the hard clay floor of the badlands that endured deep freezes in the winter and baking heats in the summer. They crossed grasslands dotted with dangling dried seedpods from the prior year.

"Loretta, come see this beauty." Brian had stepped off the trail to explore dots of color in a deep canyon shadowed by spires in the early morning. By mid-morning the area would be basking in sunlight.

"What did you find?"

"Here. There's a patch of prairie pasqueflowers, or crocus."

"They are so bold to be pushing through that dry clay. A hearty plant."

"That's why they're the state flower," Brian noted. "Sure sign of the endurance of the land and the people, I think."

"I like that. They have a handsome and strong beauty. They aren't fragile like so many of the other plants we bring into our homes and yards."

"That's true of many of the plants out here, but there are some fragile ones. Like the top of that hill over there, you'll see something called tufted evening-primrose. Last night they would've been white, like a covering of snow on the bald hill. But with the rising sun, they wilt away."

"I will have to watch for that plant the next time I'm out here in the evening. I guess I hadn't noticed that before."

"There's a lot of subtleties in the Badlands, discovered only after years of watching the patterns here."

———

THEY HIKED through a natural archway in the stone and clay formation of the Badlands, across clay, dirt, and grasses. Brian pointed out garnet beds, fossils, and other flowers including the coneflower, white sego lilies, pink woods roses, wild parsley, yellow wild peas, white prairie phlox, foxtail cactus, dark-throated shooting stars, purple thistles, soapweed, bluebells, and purple locoweed.

Loretta discovered a plant that had flowers much like the vining morning glories on the side of her house. "Hey, isn't this a morning glory?"

"That's right. It's a bush morning glory, and there, next to it, is milkvetch, and then there are all the fancy grasses that grow out here, too." Brian paused to study Loretta as she gazed out over the grasslands that carpeted this part of the Badlands floor. "Sorry, I'm probably boring you with all this information."

"Huh? Oh, no! I was just thinking about the huge differences between the way my ancestors are portrayed when they lived in these lands and the reality of what I knew of the lifestyle when I was young. It was a brutal way of life for the ancestors, moving around, depending on the bison for food and clothes and under siege by outsiders. What I experienced when I was younger on the reservation seemed so much worse than that. Looking back now, it feels like forced oppression and a loss of the fighting spirit that was so necessary as a nomadic culture historically. It's like the People's spirit was broken and only now, is starting to come out of it. Sometimes advocates from within the tribes sound so aggressive, but I'm gaining a greater appreciation for why it sounds like that. They have to be outspoken to be heard."

"Oh, I agree, and I've thought a lot about this. I don't envy you walkin' the road you do with the history of your ancestors."

"For me, it's even more personal, and someday I may tell you more. For now, just know that I had only one relative that showed me any type of love and care on the reservation. That was my grandmother, and she passed away shortly after helping me through a particularly difficult time, like she was put on earth to see that through, and then returned to what she would call the spirit world."

"Sounds like she was very special to you."

"She was, and I know every day she prayed to the ancestors to ask for wisdom, but there was a generational pain that she carried, being closer to the time of the massacres and such. Unfortunately, her daughter, my mother, never had a spiritual connection that helped her stay afloat. My mother was, as far as I can recall, an angry woman who was in survival mode. She partied all the time and hung out with rough men. Just from afar, it seems like she needed increasingly difficult circumstances to feel anything, but that's just conjecture on my part. I never really knew her."

Loretta fell into silence, surprised at how easy it was to share with Brian. She didn't want to share more…yet. Not only was there still a rawness to her new efforts to identify and connect with the child she gave up, but their relationship was young and uncertain.

The two continued to explore the Badlands. Brian shifted from describing the landscape to sharing more about himself. "I fell apart when my wife, Jerri Anne, died. I had spent so much of myself taking care of her that I was lost and missing her. After months of isolating myself and drinking way too much, my kids ganged up on me. Told me how concerned they were. An intervention that changed my life."

Loretta listened attentively and silently as Brian confided in her and shared his challenges.

"Sorry if this is too much."

"Brian, I appreciate you sharing with me. Is it okay if I ask a question?"

"Oh, sure, I'm an open book. First though, how about we take a seat on that knob over there and have a drink." He led Loretta to a baby Badland knob and invited her to sit atop the salmon-colored clay mound. "Hope you don't mind plain water. I try to stay away from too much of those artificial flavorings. Maybe I'm just a sourpuss, 'cause they just seem so sweet to me."

"You're right to be an old sourpuss," she teased, as she gladly took the bottle of fresh water. "Those drinks are unreal in the flavorings. Grape is an especially offensive fake flavor for me."

Brian held his hands up, each holding a baggie. "I have choices. Today I have brownies in this baggie. My almost daughter-in-law made them, and I'm sure they're terrific. And I have homemade gorp in this bag."

"That's a tough one. As much as I love brownies, I

think today I'll take the gorp. Now you have to tell me why she is an 'almost' daughter-in-law?"

"Because they haven't gotten married. It's the legal paper. That's the only thing. They had their wedding planned, and just put those plans on hold when Jerri Anne passed away. Maybe they will follow through and maybe they won't. I would call her my daughter-in-law, easily, but I don't want to misrepresent the truth. So she's my almost daughter-in-law." Brian chewed a mouthful of the nuts and raisins and chased the bolus with a long draw of water. He turned to Loretta, and when she made eye contact with him, he said, "And I think you had a question for me."

"Oh, yes, thanks. I was just wondering how you got to sobriety. I mean, beyond the intervention. It must have been really hard to give up the crutch of alcohol. I mean, I've seen it up close, alcoholism, that is, and it is a mighty demon."

Brian chuckled softly. "Oh yeah. Sure is. To be honest, I didn't do it alone. The first thing I did was go back to church, and not only did I just show up on Sundays, but I saw the pastor regularly, attended the extra activities, did some handyman work, and just really put myself into that environment. It felt safe to me. If I was on the church grounds, I knew I would not take a drink. That's a carry-over from my childhood and my strict, albeit hypocritical, upbringing."

"Sounds like there's a story in there."

"Sure is, and I'm happy to share some time, but I want to get back to your question, because I think it's important. People 'round me at home - my kids, my neighbors - they know bits and pieces, but only my pastor knows what that time was like for me. I would like for you to know also. I appreciate this opportunity to share with you, Loretta. I hope it doesn't feel too weird for you to be hearing this old buck sharing real talk."

"Refreshing, I would say. There's only one person in my life that knew my whole story, but he's not around anymore to share it with, and I really miss having that confidante, you know."

"I do know, and honestly, I'm not sure how I would have shared this stuff with my wife. I mean, what I went through after she died is so unlike how our life was. We were a team. We got through everything together - good and bad. Those last years, before the cancer, were great. We had a good stride, kids were all good, our business was going well, and she had a part-time job in town that let her socialize some. Really, it was going great."

Brian paused to check in with Loretta and his watch. "We can start headin' back if you want. Yah know, we've been out here nearly four hours and it will be three more, probably, for us to get back to the truck. You feel like heading back?"

Loretta checked her phone. "I see I'm not getting any signal out here. Just in case Pauline or Chance call, I think it's a good idea for me to get back into cell range."

"Good idea. They're close enough to their due date that you could be getting that special call any day now, right?"

"Yes, and I would hate to miss it." Loretta grinned.

Brian watched as Loretta smiled, face tilted toward

the sun. "Do you mind if I take a picture of you just like that? You're so beautiful, and happy."

Loretta giggled. "You'll have to be quick. I'm not much of a poser."

Brian snapped the photo quickly. "Now, can I have one of the two of us?"

"Sure, if you share it with me."

"I most definitely will." Brian scooted in beside her. "Three, two, one..."

<hr>

THE HIKE BACK to the parked pickup took just over three hours. Brian continued to share his journey to sobriety, speaking about the daily visits to his pastor, who, as it turned out, was also in recovery. "That man literally saved my life in those early days. I wasn't eating or sleeping. One day he came out to the ranch and found me unconscious on the ground. I wasn't drinking, but I was so dehydrated and exhausted that my body quit on me. He took me to the emergency room. They pumped me full of fluids, and I suppose some vitamins, and sent me on my way. For a month after that, if I didn't show up at their house for dinner by six, he was on the phone tracking me down. That month was critical for me. There's no Alcoholics Anonymous out here, but Pastor helped me work through the steps. He said that AA used to be 75 percent effective in getting and keeping someone sober and that was because the sponsor was with the alcoholic twenty-four/seven until their life was back on track. That's kinda what pastor did for me, and I haven't had a drop since."

"Sounds like it took a huge commitment and a lot of strength from you, Brian."

"What it took was a commitment to faith. All praise goes to God."

8

———

Ranch life sped up for Brian as he worked cattle, farmed, and spent countless hours manning his business…until he found himself wallowing.

"Hey, Dad!" Chad called out to his father. Brian was working under a tractor that had broken down in the summer grazing pasture.

"Hey, Chad, how are you?" Brian answered from under the tractor.

"Haven't seen you in a while. Thought I would swing by and see how it's going. Can I give you a hand?"

"Ahhh…you don't need to stand out there in the rain. I need to get this bugger fixed so I can clean up the yard around the shelter. Wait for me in the house if you want."

"Come on, the two of us working together will get you out of the rain faster. What do you need?"

Brian was silent for several moments while he wrestled with a broken pin. Finally, he spoke in a pressured voice, "Son, seriously, go on. You've seen me. I'm fine. Now get back to your own work."

Chad was alarmed. He hadn't heard his dad sound so irritable since those horrible months after his mom died. Alarmed that he might be drinking again, Chad resolved to hang out, whether Dad wanted it or not.

"You want my mallet for that job? I've got one ri…"

"No, I don't. And I don't want you standing over me in the rain. If you need something, just tell me. Otherwise, get yerself out of the rain so you don't get sick."

Steeled against his father's bad mood, Chad stood stoically silent, watching his father battle himself as much as the broken pin, under the tractor. After many clangs of the hammer against steel, grunts and barely audible curses, Brian emerged from under the tractor with mud smeared across his bare forearms and face. He pulled the tarp he was laying on out from under the tractor, rolled it into a wad, secured it with a bungee cord and tossed it in the tractor. "I see you're still here. Whatcha need, Chad?"

"Honestly? I need to know that my dad is okay. You seem a little…on edge. Anything I can do to help?"

"Here we go. You gunnin' for another intervention, son?"

"Is one needed Dad?"

"Not unless there's an intervention that will absolve me of a lifetime of regrets. I'm just in a spot, son, mullin' over the what-if's and why's of life. Can't a man just have time for reflection?"

"Of course, you can. But can't a son care about his dad's well-being and offer to be a sounding board when he's having a bad day?"

"Oh, you think this is a bad day, do you? This is one

of the better ones lately. At least I'm out here working before noon. Some days I get stuck looking through things in the house and feel trapped - paralyzed really. I can't move on. Takes me giving myself a swift kick in the butt to get to work. These cattle can't fend for themselves, really, and the crops need tending. I've got a patch of thistle over by Stark's Road that needs treating…"

"How about we get out of this rain. I'm happy to help you, but you need to tell me what I can do."

"How much time you got, son? The list might be very long."

Chad moved in and put his arm around his dad's shoulders. "Let's get on in and make a pot of coffee. We can pencil it out."

OVER A POT, or two, of coffee, Brian shared with Chad his struggle. How he was struck by waves of panic that he had not done all he could for his wife. "I could've made her more comfortable. You know, fresh sheets more often, more of her favorite foods and played more of her favorite music while she lay helpless in that darn hospital bed in the living room. If I'd moved the tv from in front of the big picture window, she would've had a better view of the ranch. One more bird feeder out there in the trees might've brought more of her favorites around."

Brian paused to refill their coffee cups. Chad sat patiently, feeling his dad's pain, but unwilling to try to talk him out of it. He knew Brian well enough to know that he would have to wade his own way through the pain for a while.

"When I'm done self-flagellating over the end, I start at the beginning and criticize myself for the honeymoon that never happened the way we dreamed, the daughter we lost through miscarriage and how I could've been more supportive. The Sundays I was too busy to go to church with her, knowing full well how important it was to her. I could go on and on, but I think you get the drift."

Brian pointed to a painting on the wall across the room. "See that picture there?"

"Sure do. That's the one Mom brought home from Paris, right? Didn't it used to hang in your bedroom?"

"Yes, that's right, but what she never shared about that picture is that I was absolutely against bringing it back with us, and it was not her first choice. The one she really wanted was two hundred dollars more and I talked her out of it."

"Why?" Chad questioned, now curious to know himself.

"Not that I didn't want her to have it, it's that I didn't want to appear pretentious, having that hoity toity impressionist painting hangin' where people would see it and feel bad because they weren't able to take a once-in-a-lifetime trip like we did. We were blessed, your Ma and I. We had our lean years, but we also had some darn good years, the kind of years ranchers dream of. On those years we bought a new car, or equipment, or took a trip. I felt badly for you mother that we had lean years and she went without."

"It's funny," Chad said. "I never heard her complain about finances."

"No, she wouldn't have. Your Ma grew up very poor. Her parents scraped by, but your grandpa always said he had a black cloud following him. It seemed to be true. There were years that his were the only crops that got hailed out or he lost cattle in a blizzard. Your grandma struggled with depression and put on a brave face every day. Their love is what kept them going all those years. It was like a gift to them when they sold out and moved into the retirement village. They never had it so good."

"Mom was always so good to them. I remember all the meals she took to them and the shuttling she did to get them to our events and to church."

"Oh, yeah, she loved and respected them, and they her. I'm sure sometimes they thought I was off my rocker, but they were never once unkind to me. They were models of what Christian love really is. I think I've lost that. I miss their influence, but not as much as your ma's. She was an angel here on earth, for sure."

The two sat in silent reflection, each in their own mind, of the lost woman in their lives. Chad was bothered by the suddenness of his father's change in demeanor. "Why now?"

"Why now, what?"

"Why is this coming up now? You've been in this place before, although much worse, I'll admit, but why is this coming up again now? What happened?"

Brian knew but wasn't sure he was ready to share with his son the inspiration for his latest self-analysis.

"That's kind of a loaded question, son. You sure you want to know?"

"Yes. That's why I asked. I think it's better to know. Maybe you can avoid the triggers in the future."

Brian let out a subtle, "Ha" and proceeded to share with his son. "I met a woman."

Brian shifted in his chair and lifted his hand, with the coffee cup dangling from his thick fingers. "Before you say a word, let me make it clear that it's not about the woman per se. She's a fine woman and I hope one day you'll get to meet her. It's because she's such a fine woman, and one I really connect with, that these things are coming up for me. Pastor says it's a natural thing, to self-reflect and 'feel the feels' as he says, but it's damned uncomfortable, especially when you've got a meddling son like mine." Brian grinned, hoping to lighten the mood for Chad's sake.

Chad grinned back. "I would think a good woman would make you feel better, not doubt yourself."

"That's just it. She's not doing it to me, I'm doing it to myself. Doing the twelve steps of AA is not a 'once and done' thing. It's like earning those degrees - a bachelor's, then a Master's, then a PhD and so on. The more one grows in their sobriety, the more nuanced the steps become and the more subtle issues there are to address within oneself. This is a new situation for me, so new things have come up for me to address. I'm fine, really, I'm just in deep contemplation. I haven't been tempted to drink and I reach out to Pastor, who is always supportive."

"It just…sounds like a lot, Dad. I'm glad I stopped in

today. Thanks for sharing with me. I might still worry, but not as much as I have been."

"You're like your ma that way. I appreciate you, son. Thanks for coming by. I really don't want to bug your brother and sister with this, so can we just keep this little speed bump to ourselves?"

"As long as you make me a promise."

"Hmm, what's that?"

"You will reach out if you're not doing well, like if you're about to have a drink, or are skipping meals, or not getting out of the house. I'll be on you, ol' man, if you do those things, and it'll be like boot camp for you."

"Woah, simmer down! I promise you I'll reach out if I find myself that low, but I really think I'm good. I've got a perspective on this thing that you can't appreciate, because you haven't been there. And honestly, it's so much better that I'm dealing with the feelings than just washing them down with whiskey."

9

---

oretta proudly shared pictures and stories of baby Lucy with the ladies gathered downtown for coffee. "She is the happiest baby I have ever held…even happier than her momma was, and Pauline was an easy baby."

"I saw the little family the other night at the hardware store," Glenda, one of the coffee crew shared. "They all looked so happy, and that Chance - I've never seen a prouder papa."

"I wasn't sure how he would react to having a little cowgirl, instead of a cowboy, but he already has plans for her goat-tying and barrel racing training." Yvette pulled her camera out to share more pictures of baby Lucy. "You're right, Loretta, our granddaughter is surely a sweet girl, and she has all that beautiful dark hair, like her momma."

THE COFFEE CREW thinned as the women left to take on their daily chores. Loretta caught Yvette by the arm and pulled her aside as they walked out the front door together. "Yvette, I have sort of a delicate question. I want to ask you, but don't want you to tell anyone I was asking. Can you do that?"

"Well, I can, unless someone is at risk for harm." Yvette patted Loretta's hand and smiled. "I know it seems like I'm a gossip queen, but I hold many confidences close, Loretta. You have my word."

"Well, I was just wondering if you guys had heard from Brian lately? I've left him a couple of text messages but haven't heard much from him since we took our hike in the Badlands several weeks ago. I mean, he did share his congratulations about the baby when she was born, but I invited him up for a visit and he hasn't responded."

"Well, we saw him, I guess a couple weeks ago, at the sale barn in Jones County, but otherwise, no, haven't heard from him. I bet he's just having a busy time at the ranch, with spring and all. Next time I hear from him, I'll have him give you a buzz."

"No, really, don't mention it to him. I'm sure he is okay. I just thought I would check in, to make sure something hadn't happened to him. I'll try calling him in the evening one day this week."

"You know, I think it's really sweet the two of you are becoming friends." Yvette spoke sincerely. "It's a good time in life for each of you to have someone who understands what the other is going through after losing a spouse."

"Thank you, Yvette. I, too, thought we were getting

on well and I appreciated having someone to talk to, but it may be too much for him."

"How do you mean?"

"Uh…" Loretta wasn't sure how much Yvette knew about Brian's journey to sobriety and didn't want to suggest he may be drinking again. "I-I just mean with all he has going on at the ranch, he may not have time."

Loretta's deeper concerns were thinly veiled. She, too, experienced questioning about seeing someone she was developing feelings for. A feeling of betraying Biggie struck her, but through prayer and quiet contemplation she realized that he would want her to be happy. She could only betray a memory of him, not he, himself, since he had already reached the other side. Besides, these days she was happily distracted by her granddaughter.

"Oh, I think I know what you're getting at, and I'm sure we would have heard from Chad or one of the other kids if there was, uh, trouble that needed tending to. He looked tired, but good when we saw him at the sale barn. All the farmers and ranchers are on high speed right now trying to get work done while the sun is shining. Please don't fret, Loretta. It's sweet the way you care, though. It gives me a warm feeling for you two. I bet if he sees you're calling, he'll answer his phone." Yvette checked the time on the bank clock and frowned. "Oh, goodness! I must check on Dan. Then I need to get out to the greenhouse. Those girls have been so busy out there and I said I would stop by to help them and help baby Annie."

"Sure, sure. Don't let me hold you up. I've got to get to work myself. I'm sure everything will work out as it should. I'll keep you posted."

"Yes, please do. We need to catch up one of these evenings when it's not so busy, or better yet, maybe I'll have a family dinner after church on Sunday. I'll let you know for sure. Love ya, Loretta. Have a great day."

Yvette and Loretta shared a warm hug before disappearing into the crowd of tourists on the sidewalk.

"HEY BRIAN. Loretta here. Just checking in here. Thought maybe we could get together for another hike or something. Give me a call back when you can." Loretta ended the call, not sure whether her feelings were out of proportion to who Brian was in her world. It was puzzling: she barely knew him, yet she seemed to know him well. They had one nice hike and several conversations by text, which she knew was the lowest form of communication, but the occasional phone calls seemed to be leading to something more. She plugged her phone into the charger, changed clothes, and headed out to work in the yard to clear her head.

"HEY MOM! I brought someone to see you." Loretta looked up to see Pauline standing in the yard holding sweet Lucy.

"Oh, my goodness. How lucky am I!" Pauline pulled the garden gloves off as she walked toward the pair. Lucy watched as her grandma approached and responded with a smile.

"We were in the city today picking up supplies. We're headed back to the ranch, but Lucy insisted she get to see Grandma, and I really need to feed her. I'm about to burst!"

"Let's go into the house. You can feed her, and I'll rustle up something for us to eat. You haven't had dinner, have you?"

"No, I haven't had dinner. That would be really nice, if it's not too much trouble."

"Of course not. Come on in." Loretta held the screen door open as Pauline carried Lucy through and sat at the kitchen table to feed her.

"It looks like the tourists are really picking up. Main Street is still lined with cars and it's after seven."

"Are you kidding? I didn't realize it was that late. I guess I got lost in my yard work." Loretta pulled leftovers out of the refrigerator and put them in the microwave to warm. "You must be starving."

"Honestly, I hadn't thought much about it, but now that I'm sitting here, I realize I am really hungry."

"I only have an assortment of leftovers. Nothing fancy, but it will fill your belly."

"I'm sure it will be great. I've always loved your cooking."

"It's pretty simple cooking, but we never starved around here." Loretta set the table and filled two glasses with ice water.

"Well, they didn't call Dad Biggie for no reason," Pauline giggled.

"Ah, yes. I sure do miss that big ol' teddy bear. He would still have been bursting with pride for who you are and all you've accomplished, and he would love this precious little baby like no other."

"I am comforted by those same thoughts. I believe he knows her and is watching over all of us."

"I agree." Loretta placed several containers on the table. "Here. A smorgasbord of culinary surprises. There's a bit of fried potatoes with onions and green peppers, some chicken and pasta concoction, coleslaw, and a homemade dinner roll."

She opened the refrigerator door. "Would you like strawberry-rhubarb jam or chokecherry jam on that roll?"

"This all looks terrific. I'll have the chokecherry, please. I'll trade you for one sleepy baby with a full tummy."

Pauline traded the jar of jam for a pacified baby Lucy, who rested comfortably in her grandmother's arms. "Have you seen Brian lately, Mom?"

"Uh…" Loretta shook her head slightly. "Nope. I guess he's busy."

To avoid further probing, she quickly asked, "So, how are you keeping up with the new baby and everything, honey?"

"How? Well, I have a superstar husband who helps me a lot and places few demands on me right now. I'm always grateful that he doesn't pressure me to go back to work, although they keep calling me. I sure wish more health care workers would be attracted to our community. There are so many people who need care of all sorts. Did you know that in the Prairie Community Assisted Living Center there are at least five people who need daily injections? When a nurse can't come down from the city, the pharmacist from the drug store goes over and gives them their shots."

"I don't know what it's going to take to attract more professionals. I suppose the clean living, fresh air, and friendly neighbors don't pay the bills. We need to be able to pay better, unless someone marries into the community." Loretta rocked the baby in her arms as she continued, "Maybe Pastor Trevor's wife, Angela, will want to help out that way."

"Maybe. I heard she already has some things lined up including training some of the small-town EMT services volunteers, teaching at the nursing school part-time in the city, and covering a couple shifts a month at the big hospital in town."

"I bet she finds herself really busy in no time. She is such a lovely woman, and of course the church ladies will want to entertain her a lot." Loretta had already heard the women of the church making plans to incorporate Angela into various church activities.

"I just hope she takes the time to be a newlywed for a while. They had a whirlwind romance and I'm sure they will one day want a family, so this is their time to establish their relationship deeper, I think." Pauline reached out to stroke her daughter's round cheek. "She is such a good baby. We are very blessed."

Loretta looked down and smiled at the baby while quietly agreeing, "Blessed, indeed."

Pauline rinsed the dirty dishes and loaded the dishwasher. "I think I should head home."

"Sure. I'll carry..." Loretta paused as she saw the

screen of her silenced phone light up and Brian's picture flash on the screen. "Oh, um…"

Pauline smiled and raced for the phone. "Maybe he's not so busy." She connected the call and continued talking, "Loretta's answering service. This is Pauline. How may I help you?"

"Well, hello, Pauline! What a pleasant surprise!" Brian cleared his throat and continued, "How is the new mother?"

"Great! I have an absolutely perfect baby." Pauline's eyes sparkled as she looked at her mother holding her daughter. "I can't wait for you to meet her. When will you be up this way again?"

"Well, I was just going to talk to your mother about that. I owe her a visit and I wondered if she was going to be available on Sunday."

"Sunday…" Pauline paused and looked at Loretta who responded with wide eyes and a furrowed brow.

"Sunday's a great day. I know for a fact that she isn't working that day. We were planning just a little afternoon barbeque starting at about one. I do hope you can join us." Pauline listened quietly and then responded. "That would be fantastic if you want to bring a pie. Great! We'll see you then. I'm going to take my baby out of Mom's hands and pass the phone over. Look forward to seeing you."

Pauline set the phone on the counter, leaned into her mother's ear and whispered, "You're welcome," as she scooped up her sleeping daughter.

"You…who are you? Now, drive safely and text me when you get home." Loretta gently hugged Pauline and kissed the baby's forehead. She waved them off with one hand while picking up the phone with the other.

"Well, I'm so sorry about that. I've never seen her be so…" Loretta searched for the right descriptor for Pauline, who seemed to have come out of her introverted shell with the birth of her daughter.

"Playful?"

"Yes, that's one way to put it. Sorry if she put you on the spot."

"Was there even a barbecue being planned?" Brian asked while softly chuckling.

"Well, maybe in her head. We hadn't actually discussed it, but I'm happy to have one. Hope you didn't feel pushed into it."

"Absolutely not. Do you have time to talk now? I've been an avoider lately and remiss in responding to you. I want to explain so there's no misunderstanding."

"Sure, can I just pour a cup of coffee while we're talking?"

"Of course. Do you need to put the phone down?"

"Nope. I am a great multi-tasker." The sound of Loretta pouring coffee could be heard in the background.

"Okay. Well, I'm sorry I haven't answered your texts and that I didn't call sooner."

"I figured you were just busy, although I was a bit worried about you, being out there alone."

"Well, thank you for that. I am alone out here, but you can be sure my kids make sure I'm okay. In fact, Chad was visiting the other day. He was worried too that he hadn't heard from me. Talking with him I was able to put words to what I've been going through and that prompted this call."

Brian went on to explain his grief process and the latest layer of personal reflection and spiritual questioning he was going through. He talked for nearly an hour, sharing stories from his married life, adventures as a family, and a recap of his drinking days. "And that brings me to us, to this call."

"Before you go any further, do you mind if I ask you a couple of things?"

"Of course not. Do you want another cup of coffee? I'm going to pour myself one."

"As a matter of fact, I do, thanks." As she walked over to refill her cup, Loretta asked, "Has it always been so easy for you to share like this, or maybe it just sounds from a distance like it's easy."

"Great question. No. With most people I'm not so open. Even when Jerri Anne was alive, I kept things from her if I thought they would be upsetting to her. No, I'd say this is unique for this time in my life and for our relationship. Even when Chad visited me, I didn't share all the perspectives and things I just shared with you. There's just such an ease I feel with you. Maybe it's because of the similarities we have with loss. Not sure, but I sure do appreciate it."

"And I appreciate you sharing all this with me. It just feels so natural to share with you, and I have to say, I was probably more worried than I let on. I was tempted to drive down and check on you myself, but I asked Yvette if she had seen or heard from you, and she assured me that they saw you at the sale barn and you were well."

"Yeah. I wouldn't feel so comfortable sharing this with her. Not much of a filter on her. I feel comfortable sharing with you, partly because I know you value the integrity of what we started here and don't have a need to reshare my story with everyone. Not the same with Yvette. I love her, but she's definitely a better fit with my brother than with me."

"I hear what you're saying. So now, you were about to tell me why you called."

"I think I just wove some of that in. I thought maybe you'd be worried, and I don't want that for you. I guess I was pretty selfish with my process, and I didn't mean to leave you in the dark anymore, wondering how I felt about you, about us, and just...things."

"So, where are we?"

"I want to keep exploring that, but with you, and not in my own head. I'd love to get some visits in so we can learn more about each other. I'm really drawn to you and think I'm ready to let someone close again." Brian paused for moment, then continued. "And where do you think we are?"

"I realize now how much I missed you when we weren't connecting," Loretta admitted. "I, too, think I'm ready to explore the world with a special someone. With you. I can't promise that I won't need to pull back and take my own time for reflection in the future, but I do think that I have healed enough to explore, so long as there aren't any expectations."

"I hear what you're saying about expectations. Yeah, I have hopes and desires, but I know expectations are a set-up for failure. Don't want to do that to either of us. I wanna get to know you better, Loretta, and your family. It was fun talking to Pauline tonight, and I can't wait to meet baby Lucy."

"I can't wait for you to meet her. She's absolutely perfect. And, by the way, what's this about bringing a pie?"

"Oh, you heard that, did you? One of the things Chad and Sam do is keep me in food. It's their excuse to keep tabs on me. I have a couple pies in the freezer that they brought me. I look forward to sharing them with y'all on Sunday."

"Awesome. I look forward to it."

"Well, Loretta, I should let you go. I know you have to work tomorrow. Once again, I do apologize for leaving you hangin' while I waded through my crap. Sure appreciate you taking time to talk tonight and look forward to seeing you Sunday."

"Me, too. Good night, Brian."

"Good night."

10

Chance was flipping burgers on the grill when Brian approached. "Hey Uncle Brian! Good to see you. How are things at the ranch?"

"Cows are great, but the crops are burning up. We are so dry down there. Seems like there's a new prairie fire every day. My neighbors had to move their cows fast one day last week. Fire started on the country road and with the winds, spread fast, straight toward them."

"Sorry to hear that. Hope they came out okay."

"You know how cows panic when they're scared. Well the neighbors got them moved to a new pasture, but not before they pushed some fence down. A few of us went over and helped fix it. That pasture burned at about eighty percent, so there'll be good grass next year, but for this summer it's pretty much a loss for them. They'll have to change up their rotation and supplements, but at least they didn't lose any cows."

"We'll be praying for rain for y'all. Seems we're always at the mercy of the weather."

"Well Chance, one thing your grandfather taught me is to never expect a high yield and to always be grateful for what's produced. There are no guarantees in this business, and we need to always save for those rainy days that will inevitably come. That means we go without a lot, but when we get a pot of gold, we can have or do something special. Get enough of those years together and you can spruce up your house, ya know."

"I've heard about Grandpa's philosophy, and I think he was spot on. Dad always framed it in terms of being able to buy Mom silk panties in the rich years. She says she hasn't gotten any yet, but we all know they have done well for themselves, silk panties or not."

Brian laughed. "You're right, Chance. Gotta be some silk panties round that ranch somewhere. Dan and Yvette have been pretty blessed over the years with a beautiful family, good health, prosperity…"

"Well, all that's true, but they can't take it for granted. I may be out of school telling you this, but Dad is struggling a bit with his health. Seems they're having a hard time controlling his blood pressure and it's damaging his kidneys some."

"Oh. Sorry to hear that. I'll have to pop in on him and see what he says. Hope they get on top of it and get him better soon."

"Yeah, well, today is not the day to dwell on that." Chance turned to his uncle with a twinkle in his eyes. "I heard you were bringing some pies up. Sam and Chad make those?"

"They sure did. I always seem to have food from them

in the freezer. Guess they worry I might not be able to fend for myself. It's kind of them, really."

"When will those two ever get married?"

"Now, that's a good question. Maybe if they do that, I could finally be a grandpa. I've seen pictures of that baby of yours and she's an absolute gem."

"She is, and her mother is an angel. Did you get a chance to hold her yet? Better go grab her from Loretta and get your turn in before you've got a burger in your hands. I think Loretta took her into the house to change her. Go on in and find them."

"Will do. I haven't seen the hostess yet. Great catching up, Chance, and thanks for grilling."

"Sure thing. Nice to see ya here." Chance smiled and returned to grilling as Brian turned away and strode toward the house.

BRIAN WALKED into the kitchen to find Pauline balancing the baby and plates on her way out to the yard. "Hi, Pauline. Good to see you. Well, there she is, that beautiful little princess!"

"Hey Brian. Glad you made it." Pauline paused for a moment beside Brian as he looked over the baby and said sweet things in baby talk.

"Wow! She really is a beauty."

"Thank you, Brian. She's a sweetheart too. We couldn't be happier. Mom should be out in a minute. She was just throwing a couple of things in the wash."

Loretta came into the kitchen. "Did I hear Brian?"

"You sure did. Hello Loretta, it's great to see you," Brian approached Loretta wanting to share a warm hug, something he had longed for since talking with her earlier in the week.

Loretta stepped back and looked up at the ruggedly handsome man. "Thank you so much for joining us. I'm happy to have you here."

Brian gently rested a hand on her wrist. "It's wonderful to see you, and your beautiful family. That baby…she is something else!"

"She is, and she's changing every day. She was born with blue eyes, and they are already starting to turn brown."

"She still has all that dark hair she was born with."

"She does, and it seems like it has grown a bunch already."

"Well, congratulations again, Grandma."

"Thanks, Brian. Should we head out and see how Chance is doing with the grill? He couldn't wait to get started."

"He always has been one to be active and stay busy."

"It has certainly served him well, all that ambition. I'm proud to have him as a son-in-law. He's a great provider for his family and could not love my daughter and Lucy any more."

"And he's lucky to have you as a mother-in-law. You bring such grace and gentleness to the world, Loretta."

"Thank you, Brian. You are very kind. There are some sodas out in the cooler, unless you want a cup of coffee."

"Soda will be just fine."

THE SUNNY AFTERNOON was filled with after-lunch fun, with neighbors stopping in for games and great conversation. Chance, Pauline and the baby left in the late afternoon, but the neighbors stayed on. Dinnertime arrived before anyone realized it, so they all pitched in for fries, shakes, and a bucket of chicken from the local drive-in.

"Brian, it's great to meet you. I guess I knew Dan had a brother, and I've heard about your athletic prowess, but it's a pleasure to actually get to know you." Loretta's neighbor, Rusty, a close friend of Biggie's, was also a high school athlete and shared many stories with Biggie before his passing. "Biggie once told me about a football game he, you, and Dan played in. I was a couple grades below you guys, so I wasn't on the team, but I remember that game. It got you into the playoffs. As I recall, you scored eight running touchdowns."

"Ah, yes, that game against North Crimpton," Brian recalled. "That was some game. One for the state athletics history books. We had four more touchdowns too. Don't recall right now what the final score was, but we held 'em down to just one or two touchdowns. Now I think I heard that you were not only a star running back in football, but you managed to go to state in wrestling too."

Rusty laughed as he shared his wisdom. "If only we knew how much we should appreciate our bodies back then, we might be in better shape at this age." He patted his distended belly. "I guess I should speak for myself. Looks like you're still in good shape."

"Ya know, I was heavy a couple years ago, but I made some changes and feel better. Trying to stay out of the doctor's office. Not much good comes from those places sometimes."

"Oh, that's right. I was so sorry to hear about your wife and all she went through. Can't imagine that was easy for you or your kids."

"Thanks. It was rough. A wonderful woman gone too soon."

"Hey fellas, we still have a couple pieces of pie over there if you care for any." Loretta pointed to the picnic table nearby.

Rusty and Brian looked at one another, laughed, and in unison responded, "No thanks!"

Brian checked the time on his phone. "I think I should probably be heading down the highway soon. Let me help you take some of these things in, Loretta."

"Thanks, Brian. That would be great."

"Sorry we didn't get much time together today," Brian said as he pulled the full bag out of the trashcan to take it outside. "I miss you when we don't get time to talk, Loretta."

"I'm still happy you got to meet the baby, and chat with the neighbors. I think everyone had a good time."

"For sure. I've always loved this town and can't believe after all the years I've been on the ranch I can still connect with locals here." He set the bag down by the door and approached Loretta. "It must be hard for you to have so many reminders of Biggie, I mean with your neighbors and all."

"Yes, sometimes it stirs my grief, but generally, I'm good. Like you, I have my moments, and there are other things in my life that come up that give me pause but I get through it."

Loretta turned away. It had been several weeks since she last saw the counselor, and she still had no response to the inquiry about the daughter she adopted out. She knew she may never hear, and now that the wound was opened again, she wondered how she would get closure. "It helps having that new baby to dote on."

Brian moved toward Loretta, who still had her back to him. He put his hand on her shoulder. "I'm a great listener, if there's anything, and I mean anything, you want to talk about."

Loretta's eyes brimmed with wetness as she responded. "That is such a great gift, Brian. I do appreciate you for that and will definitely take you up on it."

She dabbed her eyes swiftly before turning to face him. "Let's plan to get together again. Maybe go fishing? You have the more demanding schedule right now. I have seniority at work and can almost always get someone to cover for me. Let me know what's good and I'll be ready."

"Well, sounds like I need to come back up and visit my brother before too long."

"Oh? Is everything alright?"

"Chance mentioned that his dad might have some

health concerns, so I think I'll find time to corral him alone and find out what's going on. I'm going to want to do that sooner rather than later, so let me see what needs to be done at home in the next few days and I'll be back in touch, if that's okay with you. Maybe we could shoot for next weekend?"

"Sorry to hear that about Dan. Sure. You let me know what works for you. Like I say, I can manage to get almost any time off, with a little pre-planning."

"I promise, I'll be in touch this week. Thank you so much for having me over. I know it was Pauline that did the inviting and set us up, but I sure enjoyed it. More importantly, I felt welcomed and included by her, Chance, and you, and I adore baby Lucy. She's the spitting image of her beautiful grandmother."

Loretta crossed her arms and smiled. "Really, you think she favors Yvette?"

"No, Loretta, I mean you. I think she looks like Pauline who looks a lot like you. You are beautiful women. I'm sure Chance would agree. Own it, my friend."

Loretta looked to the spotless kitchen floor, cheeks warming with embarrassment. She wasn't used to such compliments. "Thanks, Brian."

11

———

oretta wiped sweat off her forehead with the back of a hand. "This is great exercise."

"But not much of a date. This is probably the first date in history that involves weeding a garden and harvesting produce. I know it's a first for me."

"Well, there's a first time for everything, and I appreciate the opportunity to work outside. Could you pass me that water bottle, please?"

Brian stooped to pick up the bottle. "Coming at ya!" he called out as he tossed it.

"Thanks." Loretta took a long refreshing drink. "Remind me what all you do with this produce you don't use."

"Did ya see that little stand at the end of the driveway when you turned into the yard here? For the hardier produce, I just set it out and whoever needs it in the community knows it's there. If there's quite a lot, I take a picture and Sam posts it on some Facebook page or passes it around, so people know to come out. I'm a little off the beaten path so many of the takers are passing through on their way back to the reservation or into town, but it is unlikely that a tourist would wander by and find the stand of free stuff."

"What about the more fragile stuff, like these greens? They're ready for harvest but I'm thinking they probably won't last long in the heat on the stand."

"There's actually a refrigerator plugged in out there. But to be on the safe side, I set them out at church on Sunday morning and they disappear. I'll pick today, rinse it all, dry it, bag it and take it in tomorrow."

"That's really kind of you, to share like that."

"You can't credit me. Jerri Anne actually started it many years ago and it's just one of the things I try to keep up in her honor."

"What a great heart she must have had."

"She was very kind-hearted. This life on the ranch can be darn harsh at times. Sometimes I worried she was too timid for the harshness, but she grew into it, especially after having the kids. She developed an assertive side, like a lot of mothers do."

"We are just protecting our cubs, you know."

"And y'all do it well. But I can't imagine you laying into anyone."

"Don't let my size and quiet nature fool you," Loretta warned. "You cross me regarding my family, and I will be all over you."

"Yikes! Has that ever happened? When your hackles were really up, and you went all out fight mode?"

Loretta skipped over the thoughts about being raped and forced to give up a child, and launched into an animated description of an event involving Pauline. "Pauline experienced bullying before it was ever a thing in schools. I mean, nobody was watching for it or coaching the kids on what it means."

"It's darn terrible, this bullying stuff."

"It really is, and what was happening to Pauline happened on the playground, so the teachers and administration were barely aware of it. It got so bad that in second grade she didn't want to go back to school."

"What were they doing to her?"

"Some of the kids drew a line across the playground. They chased her into a tiny dirt corner and told her she lived on the 'rez' side of the line, in the little corner of dirt, and she couldn't come into the rest of the playground without asking permission and crawling on all fours across the line."

Brian was shocked. "That's horrible. How did kids even get ideas like that?"

Loretta's face held a look of bitter disgust. "Where do you think? They get it from their homes, which just amplified my anger."

"So, what did you do?"

"Well, I didn't tell Biggie till later; he would've beat those kids bad. First thing I did was let her stay home and found her a counselor to talk to right away. One who wasn't involved in the school system. Then, I confronted every teacher that had playground duty, which was every teacher. They didn't seem to notice this was going on, which was a problem in itself. Then, I talked to her classroom teacher about changes in Pauline's demeanor in class."

"What did that teacher say?"

"He said he noticed she was quieter but assumed there were issues at home."

"Oh, no!"

"Right?! I came unglued and let him have a piece of my mind, and I didn't stop there. There was obviously a series of problems that weren't being addressed. I marched into the superintendent's office. She was very gracious to give me the time and space to rant. As it turned out, she had been trying to get anti-bullying curriculum into the school, but most school board members didn't see a need for it. We devised a plan for me to present my story to the school board at their next meeting and she invited the author of the curriculum to co-present and describe how the curriculum would help solve the problems I identified."

"Brilliant! So, what happened?"

"At first, the school board wasn't very receptive. But then, as part of my presentation, I presented them with a letter from an attorney I consulted, and bills for Pauline's therapy. I mean, I hated to reveal that she was in counseling, for her sake, but I knew that the threat of a lawsuit and potential fiscal impacts would be useful to persuade them, if necessary."

"And it obviously became necessary."

"As it turned out, the lead bully was the son of a board member. That apple didn't fall far from the tree. First, the guy wasn't going to let me on the agenda, but he was overruled. Then, he tried to pass it all off as 'kids will be kids' until I spewed a bunch of data at him from research on bullying behaviors and where they originate."

"Did Pauline recover okay?"

"You don't necessarily forget such an attack on your personhood, but it didn't ruin her. It made a big difference that I was there for her and believed her. So many kids don't get that level of support at home and that compounds the trauma for them so much."

Brian moved in closer to Loretta, inspecting the spinach leaves she was weeding. "I had no idea you were such a psychologist."

Loretta laughed and responded, "I'm no psychologist, but I'm a reader. I've read a lot on trauma and, well, to be honest, I've had my own trauma and have worked with a therapist to deal with it."

She looked away from Brian, feeling embarrassed and surprised to be revealing this much of herself.

"Therapy was one of the things that saved me when I hit bottom," Brian admitted. "I've a lot of respect for those people, willing to listen to the problems of others and help them solve some of the most horrific situations and losses. My circumstances, my trauma, so to speak, was nothing like what a lot of folks go through, but I surely did need help to dig out of my dark hole. Between my pastor and my counselor, I somehow found daylight and crawled towards it again."

"That's a great description of what happens," Loretta said. "I have learned to recognize when life starts to dim, and get a little help then, before everything goes dark. It's a useful tool, and one I'm no longer embarrassed about using."

"Amen. I like the way you think, Loretta." He paused for a moment, and waited until she turned to look at him before continuing. He pointed a grimy gloved finger at her. "In fact, I really like you. I'm so grateful for this chance to learn more and more about you. What an exciting date, huh? Working in the garden."

"I can honestly say that working in the garden is one of my happy places, so no regrets here," Loretta replied while stuffing a plastic bag with pruned fresh spinach leaves. "Some lucky person is going to make a beautiful salad or something out of this."

"I sure do hope so. They could put it in a flaxseed smoothie, for all I care. I just hope somebody uses it."

"Have you had one?"

"One what?"

"Flaxseed smoothie."

"Oh. Well, I did try one once." He crinkled up his nose. "It was really green and tasted like chlorophyll. Can't say it was my favorite."

"I don't think I would care for that either. I have to say, Pauline and I have made up some good concoctions using fruit. Maybe you'll give it another try sometime?"

"I just might. We can put it on our list of future adventures."

"Sounds good," Loretta agreed. "What else would be on that list of adventures?"

"How about a concert? How'd you feel about that?"

"I would feel great, so long as it's not rap. I love live music, but not all of it makes my heart sing."

"Hah! No rap here. I'm a country boy. I'll be on the lookout for something good. What else should go on the list?"

"Okay. Um, how about fishing. I would like to see fishing on the list, more than once even."

"Fishing it is. Sounds great, but probably not at the height of summer. Better in the fall if we want to go to the streams in the hills." Brian started gathering up the garden tools. "I think we can take the harvest into the house now and wash 'em up."

"Perfect." Loretta followed Brian toward the house while contemplating their evolving list. "Another thing I would love to do with you is go horseback riding. I am not a skilled rider. I've only done a couple trail rides. Could we put that on the list?"

"Sure thing. That'll go on the list, along with meeting the kids, and time with family." He slowed down a bit. "Speaking of family, stopped by Dan and Yvette's one afternoon last week. Expected to have to search the ranch for Dan, but didn't have to. He was having a siesta on the porch. Steve and the hands were covering for him for a few hours and Yvette was in town picking up supplies."

"That's strange," Loretta spoke with concern. "Don't think I've ever seen Dan rest, or trust Yvette with picking up supplies alone."

"Yeah," Brian agreed. "Says he's been feeling kinda crappy, tired and sore, and more than happy to let the others do some work. Had a few laughs over growing older but not wiser, remembering the craziness of younger years and younger bodies."

"I'm glad you had that time with him. Haven't seen Yvette around much lately. Dan's always so helpful with everyone else, and it's such a busy time of year in these parts. Bet it's hard for him to grow old and slow down.

Hope he sees a good doctor. Adding him and Yvette to my prayer list, and maybe get a visit in."

"Yeah, same here. Say…how 'bout adding dinner out with Dan and Yvette to our list? Or maybe a getaway - some trips like somewhere south in the winter?" Brian looked at Loretta and smiled. "Does any of that sound good to you?"

Loretta smiled back. "Yep, I like your ideas. I'm looking forward to hearing more about them."

12

The ease with which they worked together in the garden continued in Brian's kitchen.

"How 'bout some of these fresh veggies for dinner?" Brian asked comfortably. "Loretta, I was thinking maybe you might stay over and go to church with me tomorrow. Help me deliver those greens."

"What will your friends say? What about Chad and Sam?"

"Heck, I don't really care 'bout what they think or say. I have a spare room or three. I'm not suggesting anything other than a nice dinner, more great conversation, and a trip to church in the morning. No pressure here, Loretta. I've just enjoyed our day together so much that I don't want it to end." Brian rinsed the last of the veggies and laid them out to dry. "If you feel uncomfortable, I understand and won't bug you anymore. Just know it's an option."

"Thanks, Brian. I would love to, but, uh, I think it would be better if we spent a bit more time together before we filed into the same pew in your small-town church. I mean, I just don't want to rock the boat for you until we, well, until we, uh, until we know what WE are." Loretta paused and thought about her words. "I don't mean to be a contrarian here. I just think we both deserve to be thoughtful and enjoy our exploration before we invite the world into it."

"Now that makes a lot of sense. You can tell I'm a pretty passionate kind of guy. Sometimes I feel like I'm bursting with emotion and just want it all out there, but what you're saying is wise."

"Thanks for hearing me. It's a new space for each of us to be in. It's not like our youth where we lived our lives out loud and proud, mistakes and all. I think we have others' feelings to take into consideration…"

"Yeah, like our children…"

"That's right, and those who have been there for us. I mean, you probably want the opportunity to introduce me to your children, or at least give them some runway that lets them know I exist."

"Yup. Sounds good. But, can you stay for dinner? Or do you think it'll get too late to drive back if we make some dinner together?"

"I'm game for dinner, for sure. I worked up an appetite and…" Loretta fluffed the spinach and lettuce leaves drying on the counter. "Who could pass up these super fresh greens in a beautiful salad?"

"Yahoo! I've got some shrimp or some beef. I can do up a pasta and veggie dish while you make the salad."

"Sounds perfect."

"So what'll it be? Shrimp or beef. Or both? Don't matter to me."

"I think this feels like a shrimp night."

DINNER PREPARATION WAS A FUN EXPERIENCE, with easy conversation. They listened to music, each calling out to the Alexa device for their favorite music. Country and contemporary Christian filled the room. Brian seasoned the shrimp and put them on the grill while the pasta boiled.

"You are quite the talented chef, Brian. I'm impressed."

"Don't be yet. You haven't tried it. I like watching those cooking shows on TV in the winter. Learned a few signature dishes from that. I keep that a secret though. Don't want people to have high expectations of my culinary abilities."

"You're funny! Thanks anyway. It's a new experience to have someone cook for me, and I think I like it."

"It's new for me, too. Jerri Anne did all the cooking until she couldn't anymore. I was able to put a few things together for her, but we never really cooked much together. She was skilled at making meals the kids would eat and she taught the boys to cook, too. She wanted them to be able to look after their own needs. They're good housekeepers, too."

"That's great. Yvette was the same with her boys. It's not a big deal for Chance to take over in the kitchen and let Pauline sit with the baby. He might even be a better cook than she is. She was never too interested in making fancy things. She's getting better, and can make a mean breakfast for dinner meal, but fettuccini alfredo is probably not in her repertoire yet."

"Well, it might be beyond my kids, too. Truth be told, it was never served in this house until I learned to make it from a TV show last year. So far, I'm the only one who's eaten it here." He chuckled mischievously. "You'll be the second. Hope you live to tell about it."

"THAT WAS A FANTASTIC MEAL, Brian. And I am alive to tell about it."

"Thank the Lord!" Brian laughed. "Sorry I don't have any dessert for us."

"Oh, I had two helpings of pasta. There is no way I could have also had dessert."

"The salad was wonderful. Good job tossing that together for us."

"Whoever takes those greens home from church in the morning is in for a real treat. They are so fresh and filled with flavor."

"Can't beat fresh."

"Here, let me help you get things…"

Brian reached across the table and put his hand on Loretta's. "Loretta, would you mind taking a walk with me? I've made a habit of walking out along the bluff in the evening. Sometimes I can see an elk, or a coyote wandering through. If I go close to sunset, God can deliver a real treat with a dramatic sky. We won't see that tonight, it's a little early, but we might see something. I'll do the dishes later."

"I'm happy to take a walk but feel bad about leaving you with the clean-up."

"Ah, don't worry about it. I suspect there'll be future opportunities to help with clean-up here. At least I hope so." Brian took the pasta dish to the counter. "I'm going to send you off with some leftover pasta though. I'll just box it up and put it in the fridge while we take a walk."

"That would be lovely. I'm happy to take it home with me. I'll enjoy it tomorrow, I'm sure. I probably don't need a jacket, right? The sun's still up."

"Yeah, that's right. But when we step outside, spray for mosquitos if you want to. They can be brutal."

"How long have you been working this land?"

"I came out here just after college. Jerri Anne and I met in college, married the same year we graduated, and then we moved out here. Her parents had some health concerns, and the place was falling apart so we moved an old travel trailer out here and started working the place. She taught school, and helped out on the ranch as well. When her folks had to go into supervised living, we took on the house as a project and eventually moved into it. By that time, our oldest was born and we needed the extra space."

"Did your wife have any siblings?"

"No, sadly. As I understand it, there were many miscarriages and broken hearts, which probably didn't help her parents' physical health any. Don't get me wrong. They loved Jerri Anne with all they had, but I think they would've been happy to have a bigger family and Jerri Anne would have been a great sister. So, they gave her all they could, and loved our family 'til the end. We had regular dates to take them to church and out here. Jerri Anne had them visit with the children as often as she could. We stopped bringing them out to the ranch when it got too difficult for them. They both ended up with dementia and even stopped recognizing Jerri Anne in the end. For some reason, they seemed to remember me."

"That must have been heartbreaking to experience."

"It was terrible. But we don't live each day wondering what the end of our lives will be like. As hard as it is to let a loved one go, I think it's more cruel to perpetuate their suffering. Jerri Anne took treatment for her cancer the first two times she had it, but by the last time, she decided the suffering of treatment was too much to put herself and the family through. I regret that there were no grandchildren before she passed, but she will eventually meet them on the other side."

Standing on the bluff overlooking the small clay mounds of the edge of the Badlands below, Brian turned to Loretta and took her hands in his. "That's enough of this morbid talk. Loretta, I'm so glad you came out to spend time with me today. It's been a real joy to work beside you in the garden and the kitchen. I feel like we dance well together. I hope it wasn't too boring for you."

Loretta stepped in a bit closer to respond. "I wasn't bored at all. I felt right at home all day. It's amazing that I don't feel judged or pressured when I'm with you.

Hanging out with you is like wearing an old comfortable shirt and jeans, if that makes sense."

Brian moved closer, his face dropping down toward Loretta's as she looked up to him. "Sure does. Loretta, I want to kiss you, would that be alright?"

His head dipped lower and his lips touched hers before she had a chance to respond, but she made no effort to move away from his advance. After a long, passionate kiss, Loretta pulled back slightly and whispered, "Yes."

The sun floated above the horizon, streaming light across the colorful mounds of the Badlands, showing off their variegated colors of buff, copper, and faint green. Birds hopped amongst the wild grasses waving in the breeze. Sounds of calves calling to their mothers floated in the distance as the couple enjoyed another deep kiss and merging embrace.

13

"Hi, Loretta. Sorry I missed you. I'm going to be in town on Saturday. Got an invite from Yvette to join them for a family dinner. I wondered if maybe I can see you while I'm in town. I'd invite you, but it wasn't clear that this was that kind of dinner, where I could bring a plus one. Hope you're having a great day at work. It's fine to just text me back. I'm sure we'll talk soon."

Loretta listened again to Brian's message. She, too, had received an invitation from Yvette for the same family dinner. The invitation came by text and Yvette had been missing from morning coffee all week.

Loretta put her phone away and turned to help a customer. At the height of tourist season, personal calls were nearly impossible to sneak in and breaks were hard to come by. After the last guest purchased the last ridiculously over-priced and uninspired t-shirt of the day, she locked the door and quickly dialed Pauline.

"Hi, honey. How was your day? How's that precious granddaughter of mine?"

"Hey, Mom. All is well here. Busy, of course. Chance has been away quite a bit this week, supporting some of his young cowboys getting ready for competitions. Baby Lucy is great, as always. She's starting to coo more and loves being outside."

"And you, honey? How are you? Getting enough rest?"

"Yes, I'm feeling good. This is my prime time of year. I love it when I can spend the days outside. It's not quite harvest yet and the livestock is all well, knock on wood. I miss Chance when he travels like this. I'm thinking Lucy and I will be on the road with him when he travels this fall."

"Oh, good. I'm glad all is well. Say, I was just wondering, do you know what the occasion is for this family dinner on Saturday? Yvette didn't really say, and we're not to bring anything. It's not their anniversary, and it's nobody's birthday that I can think of."

"No, I don't know. But they were very insistent that all the kids were home, so Chance is cutting his roping clinic a little short that day so he can drive back from Wyoming and be home in time for dinner."

"I heard from Brian that he is coming up, too, and they also invited me. I just kind of have a little bit of a bad feeling." Loretta was walking toward home, dodging strangers on the sidewalk as she wove through the town's summer visitors.

"You know, I do, too, but I'm not asking any

questions. I'm going to hope I'm being worried over nothing, and all is well."

"I like your attitude and think I will do the same. Let's just keep them in our prayers."

"Yes, of course."

"Well, I love you, my dear. Kiss the baby for me. I'll see you soon, and on Saturday for sure."

"Talk to you later, Mom. Have a great evening."

Yvette stood on the expansive deck looking south over the Badlands, greeting the family guests. The summer sun still reigned down from the clear western sky.

Brian had waited in the driveway for Loretta to arrive. Cowboy hat in hand, he leaned in and kissed Loretta's blushing cheek as she stood and closed the car door behind her. "My, it's nice to see you."

"Hello, Brian. It's great to see you too. Any idea what's going on here? I feel so odd coming with empty hands. Usually, I am here to help or bring a dish or a gift or something."

"I am just as much in the dark as you are, honestly. I've got an uneasy feeling…"

"Oh, me too. I've been praying over Dan and Yvette, hoping they are okay, but that feeling has not gone away since the moment I got their invitation."

"Same here. Let's put on our brave faces and join them, shall we?" Brian extended the crook of his arm and they walked together toward Yvette.

"Welcome, Brian and Loretta. So glad you could join us this beautiful evening."

Lorretta leaned in to hug her friend. "You've got great weather tonight, Yvette."

"I ordered it up special. Sometimes, God answers our prayers in a way we expect to see them answered." Yvette paused and looked toward the house and across the family coming together on the deck before continuing. "And sometimes, he doesn't. You two take any seats you want. Dan's hanging out over by the food with Belle and Steve. They're helping me cook and serve tonight. We've got mostly family here tonight, and a couple others. You'll see Trevor and Angela, Kerry's mom, Susan, and a few others in our circle. There's iced tea, pops, and water in the coolers. Help yourself."

Brian ushered Loretta to an empty table with room for Pauline and Chance, who were nowhere in sight yet. "How's this? We can hold these places for Pauline, Chance, and the baby."

"That'll be lovely."

Brian pulled out a chair for her. "Can I get you a drink?"

"Yes, thank you. Ice tea sounds great. It's still pretty warm out here." Loretta spotted pastor Trevor and Angela a couple of tables away and waved. They smiled and returned the greeting.

Loretta watched as Brian greeted Stella, who had flown in from Arizona. He stopped by Dan's table, greeted him and shook his hand. Moving around the deck, he said "hello" to those he knew, which was nearly everyone. He returned to the table with drinks and a perplexed look.

"So, how's everyone?" Loretta anxiously greeted Brian as he returned to their table. "Dan's looking a little tired."

"Ah, yeah, a little tired and preoccupied, but otherwise seems fine." Brian took a drink of his water. "Oh - I see Pauline. Let me go see if I can help them carry anything."

"You're so kind. Thanks." Loretta smiled as Brian greeted first Chance with a hearty handshake, then Pauline. She could see him smiling and talking to baby Lucy. Her heart was full.

<hr>

Pauline and Chance were the last guests to arrive. Once they were settled, Yvette greeted everyone and thanked them for being there. She asked Pastor Trevor to bless the meal, then instructed everyone to fill their plates and eat up.

"Well, this all seems a bit mysterious," Chance said while scanning the guests on the deck. "This is an interesting mixture of old friends and family. How 'bout you, Uncle Brian, you good?

"Yup, doing good here. Your dad seems a bit tired. You seen him lately? He doin' okay?"

"Haven't seen much of him this summer. He was feelin' poorly over the spring and hasn't quite bounced back." Chance watched as Brian stood to escort the guests from his table to the serving table before joining them. As the minutes passed by, he felt more and more uneasy. Tension and anxiety grew in him. He wasn't sure he would be able to eat, but at Yvette's continued urging, they all filled their plates and sat down.

"I know it's warm out here," Yvette said. "But please, fill up your plates. Dan and I will be chatting with you all after a bit here. Eat. Eat. There's enough food here for an army."

AFTER PUSHING the food around on his plate, Brian got up from the table. He side-stepped the serving table to talk with Steve, who seemed to be the closest to his parents these days. He hoped to gain some insights into the strangeness he felt. "Hey, Steve, need any help here?"

"Oh, hey Uncle Brian. No, I'm doing okay here. Just finishing up grilling the extras in case someone wants seconds, or thirds. You're looking pretty trim there. I don't suppose you'll be double-dipping tonight?"

"Thanks, man. I'm doing alright, and no, I probably won't be. Say, do you know what's going on here?"

"Sorry, Uncle, this is their night. I'm just the cook. I have some ideas but am about as clueless as the rest of you." Steve nodded toward the serving tables. "Get yourself another plate and fill it up. You don't want to upset the hostess."

"I'll do that. Thanks. You, too?"

"Right behind you there."

SUBDUED CONVERSATION FILLED the air as the group ate. Then Yvette stood behind Dan's chair and clanked a glass with a spoon for attention. With a look of firm determination, she faced the group gathered together. "Friends and family, thank you for joining us today. I'm happy to hear all the conversation but want your attention now for a little bit. I know you're curious about today's occasion because, well, we usually have something we're celebrating when we call our friends and family together. Today is a little different. I know, because you've asked, that you're wondering what's going on. Well…" Yvette moved beside Dan's chair and waited while he stood up before continuing. "Here's Dan to share some words with you."

As Dan stood, someone moved to the empty chair next to where Dan stood. Brian whispered into Loretta's ear, "That's Doc Bell with him. What the hell?" She turned toward him, her face frozen with a furrowed brow.

"Hey Dad!" Chance shouted, out after a moment of stunned silence. Several calls of "Hi, Dan" followed from the group.

Dan raised his hand to wave, appearing a little shaky. With a slightly quivering voice, he addressed the assembled loved ones. "Thanks for being here today. Nice to see you all. I can just hear all the whispers going on out there, and I imagine if you all are whispering, the whole town of Buffalo Ridge is. Hell, probably even the entire county. Some things haven't changed. You all know I grew up out here on the edge of the Badlands. I've spent hundreds of nights like tonight hanging out under this beautiful sky, which later will grace us with the dance of the stars."

Dan paused and looked at his guests. "Yvette, could you hand me some tea?"

Yvette picked a glass up off the table and put it in his hand. He took a long sip as he faced family and friends, prepared to make one of the most difficult disclosures of his life.

"What I have to say to y'all tonight is hard, even for me, a tough ol' cowboy who has seen a lot. I've weathered drought and famine, stillborn calves and blight. I've danced with joy in rains, rejoiced when my kids were born healthy, calves too. One thing we've done right, 'Vette and I, is to stay close with our family and our friends. That's why we wanted y'all to join us tonight. Ya see, I've been kinda sick. Most of you have noticed I haven't quite been on my game recently."

Guests shifted in their chairs. Pauline looked to Chance while Loretta reached out to rest a hand on Brian's. He massaged her hand with his thumb as they sat in silence, waiting for the pending bad news.

"The thing is the Lord's been really good to me, but I still got some challenges to face. I have something they call ALS. Or maybe ya heard of Lou Gehrig's disease."

Dan paused for the audible gasp amongst the group.

"Oh, hold on to your shorts. It ain't that bad. See me, I'm still Dan and I'm still up here yackin' yer ear off. We ain't going to tears and worries here, and I mean it."

Yvette rubbed Dan's back as she addressed the group. "The thing is, we've got this. We Davies are no wimps.

Dan's here talkin' to y'all and you can see he's doin' good."

"That's right, darlin'. We're good, our family's great, and we keep truckin' along. But we aren't stupid. We know our lives will change over time. This thing that I've got is gonna take a long time to usher me into my grave, but along the way, you're gonna notice some things. Already my hands shake and sometimes my feet get heavy. Those things'll get worse. I think the most heartbreaking thing is I'm eventually not going to want to eat much, and y'all know how 'Vette likes to feed me." A ripple of nods and quiet giggles passed through the group.

"Can't blame a gal for tryin," Yvette retorted.

"Well, anyway, we're just tryin' to git ahead of the rumor mill we all know is out there. Yes, I've got a little something. No, I'm not dying anytime soon. And by God yes, we still believe in Jesus." Laughter and smiles ensued. This was the Dan whom they knew and loved. "Y'all may have noticed that I brought my ol' pal Doc Bell in tonight. We've been buds for a long time and both enjoy being Buckaroos. Anyway, good ol' Doc agreed to answer any and all questions you might have. Well, not all, maybe. Some things 'Vette and I like to keep to ourselves."

As Dan sank to his seat, Doc Bell stood and spoke. "Hi y'all. For those who don't know me, I'm Doc Bell, an old country doc from these parts and a longtime friend of the Davies family. My wife, Elaine, is sitting over there with Steve and Bella's family." Elaine waved in acknowledgement. "I was invited today by Dan and Yvette, to share their, well, rather tough news.

"Y'all haven't seen Dan out in the fields or downtown too much recently. He's been feeling poorly for a bit. It started last spring with him feeling kinda run down and he had some muscle tremors that were new for him. We did a bunch of tests and couldn't find anything wrong. Dan, being the trooper he is, kept working and Yvette, being the loving wife she is, kept trying to feed him and help him with chores and things, but Dan just couldn't seem to get over this thing. We got them a spot at Mayo a couple of weeks ago for some consultations and more tests. Dan just shared with you what those tests told us."

Doc Bell paused and looked to Yvette and Dan. "Before I answer any questions you might have, I want to say that these are two of the finest people I know. They work this land with the utmost care, have raised their family with boundless love, and have contributed to this community with their heart and soul. Now, it is our turn to repay them. They have a long journey ahead of them. You were called here today because you have a special place in their world, and they in yours. They wanted to get ahead of the rumor mill and have extended family and special friends around to support their children and them at this time."

Pauline hugged the sleeping baby Lucy closer, as she listened to the news of her father-in-law's illness. As a healthcare worker, she understood the gravity of the diagnosis and the challenges ahead.

Doc Bell fielded questions about how this group could best help Dan and the Davies family. He explained the progressive way Dan would lose functioning and finished with the good news. "Dan started this journey as a very healthy, active man and that will be of great benefit to him."

Yvette stood and again addressed the group, "Thanks, Doc Bell. You can see why I wanted the scientist to bring the details. It's a complex thing Dan's going through. You all know us; know we are faithful people and are praying for the best outcome possible. We also live off the land, close to nature, and have seen diseases run their course."

She reached out and stroked her husband's face. "We've noticed that Dan does get tired earlier these days, so we need to pace ourselves. We also need to pace ourselves because this is a long, long marathon. Now we know the dear people of Buffalo Ridge are going to be inquiring. It's fine to share what you heard here, but please know, and Dan and I mean this from the bottom of our hearts, we do not see this as the end of the world. We see this as something God has delivered to us as a way for us to serve others. Now, mind you, we don't know all the how's and why's of that yet, but we firmly believe it and will be living every day with that in mind."

Yvette and Dan finished with a heartfelt thank you to all those present, and assurances that they were available for summer picnics and drinks on the deck.

14

————

*L*oretta handed a cup of freshly brewed coffee over to Brian and sat across the coffee table from him. She slid a plate of cookies to the center of the table, inviting him to take one. "That was a lot to take in. How are you doing, Brian?"

Brian took a long drink of coffee. "Well, I'm full from dinner so don't need cookies. Otherwise...don't know how I'm doing."

"So, I just have to ask. Did you see this coming? I mean, did it seem like Dan was that sick to you?" Loretta dunked a chocolate chip cookie into her coffee then let it dissolve in her mouth.

Brian sat deep in thought for a minute before answering. "You know how you just have a feeling sometimes?" He shook his head and rolled his eyes. "Look at who I'm talking to. Of course, you know. I had a feeling something more serious was wrong when I caught him napping that afternoon. Then when they went to the Mayo clinic, I really knew something wasn't right, but

114

we've always honored one another's privacy and I had to wait. He has shown me such patience and grace over the years that I want to show him the same. So, short answer, yes, I thought something was going on, but woah… definitely not this."

"I thought it was kind of interesting that they told everyone at once. Did it seem awkward to you, as a close family member?"

"At first, I had a twinge of feeling left out. Cripes, I'm his brother! But thinking 'bout it now, I can see why Yvette and Dan, being who they are, did it that way. They don't want to have to keep telling the story over and over again. This way, the news is out there. Enough of us have the facts that we can correct any rumors or false gossip, and Dan and Yvette can focus on the important things. They'll want to look forward and not get mired in the muck of the diagnosis and prognosis."

"I bet everyone that was there today is home now googling for more information, but really, what we need to do, in my humble opinion, is to be available for them when they need us. Eventually we may be able to anticipate their needs, but for now, I think we really just need to watch and listen." Loretta reached behind her, pulled a pillow onto her lap, and hugged it tight. She recognized this as a habit and presumed it was protective in some way. When she rose to freshen the coffee, she dropped the pillow on the rocking chair across the room. This was a silent and intimate gesture of increasing her vulnerability.

"And send up lots of prayers. You know that couple has friends all over this country and a prayer chain could do a lot of good. That's one way we could help, for now." Brian sucked down the last gulp of coffee so Loretta could refill his cup.

"Brilliant. I will be sure it gets started at the churches here in town and before long it will be all over Facebook and you can bet some of those folks will take it to prayer." Loretta sat back down, sans pillow, and thought about the night. Turning to Brian she asked, "And you, Brian, what can I do for you? This situation must stir up a lot in you."

"See, that's what I love about you. You're always thinking of how you can help others." Brian swallowed hard and looked to Loretta for a reaction.

"I think we are much alike in that way, Brian. But I'm not sure that I deserve your love just for that."

Loretta crossed her legs, crossed her arms, and let her hands grasp her thighs. Even without the pillow, her posture was protective.

"You don't have to DO anything to be loved by me, Loretta. It is who you are that stirs my heart. I know I haven't said the L word before, but believe me, I've felt it since that first hike in the Badlands, and maybe even before that. Out there, where we were able to talk freely and share a love for nature, I felt a warmth spread from my heart outwards and it has only grown since that time."

Loretta's body unfolded and she turned away to brush a tear from her cheek. Brian recognized the gesture and rose from his seat. He knelt beside her chair and took her hands. "Honey, what is it? You look so forlorn right now. It's been a roller coaster around here and tonight was a pretty big low, but I didn't mean to make you cry."

"Brian, if you only knew all about me, I don't think you would feel the same."

"Try me. I've got all night and I'm a patient man. When you are ready, you can tell me anything." He reached for a footstool and shifted, making himself comfortable for the duration.

Loretta reached for a tissue to wipe her face, which was now wet with tears. After a long pause, she wiped her eyes one last time and turned to Brian. "I'm afraid this may be too much for you, and I wouldn't blame you. You see, my friends don't even know this about me."

"Loretta, do you trust me? I care so much about your heart and your happiness, there's nothing you can tell me that will change that."

"Yes, I trust you, but you don't need to hear this after the news you just got about your brother. It seems so selfish of me to even make it a thing right now."

"You know as well as I do, we don't time our outpouring of grief any more than we can schedule when we fall in love. I love you, Loretta. That you can be sure of. It hurts me to see you swallow your secret so hard when you have an opportunity to share with me and lift your burden." Brian reached up and gently stroked her face. "I'm here for you and if you don't want to tell me tonight, I can just sit here in silence with you. One day, you'll be ready to share."

With a deep sigh and new resolve, Loretta plowed forward. "It might as well be now. This secret has come up in me several times since Pauline got pregnant and I've dealt with the shame of it through counseling. As a secret, though, it holds some power and I've felt a need to retain that power for some reason. Sharing with you, I don't really fear being judged anymore, as I didn't do anything wrong, but I do worry that it may stir emotions in others that I don't want to deal with."

"You don't have to tell anyone, Loretta. I'm cool with that. If you do choose to tell me, you have my word that I will not share with anyone else, and my word is golden."

Loretta thought on his offer. She reflected briefly on the counselor's encouragement to dissipate the hold the secret had on her by confiding in one other person who was important in her life. Brian was that person right now.

"Okay, I will tell you, but you need to go sit back on the couch. You look terribly uncomfortable sitting on that short stool."

Brian squeezed her hand and followed her instructions. He moved to the end of the couch nearest the recliner where she sat, within touching distance. Loretta began her story. She described her early life on the reservation with chaos at home and a safe haven provided by her grandmother. "I didn't know that life wasn't like that for everyone. I mean, my friends were in the same boat. We would sometimes sneak out and share whatever we could get our hands on in the house while our parents partied. Eventually we figured out that we could slip in and out of the bedroom windows. One day my dad discovered the stack of wood I set up leading to the window and threw the logs all around the yard, nearly hitting my friend and me. He said, 'No daughter of mine is going to be sneaking out of her bedroom window. I don't care who you think you are, you are not going to be roaming around these streets. I know what happens to little girls who do that.'"

"So what happened after that?"

"Initially, he boarded the window shut, but it wasn't too long after that when he and my mom got in a huge fight. She had to go to the hospital and social services stepped in. There were five of us kids. We were all split up. I desperately wanted to go to my grandmother's, but she could only take one of us and that was my youngest sister who was a baby at the time. Somehow, I was designated the troublemaker. I mean, I was only six, but I was the oldest girl, and the one dad was mad at. I went to live with the itinerant pastor and his wife. Before the next school year started, they shipped me off to boarding school on the other end of the state."

Loretta caught her breath. Her body was tight from reliving the chaos of that time. She retrieved the pillow from across the room, hugging it like a long-lost friend. "Boarding school was good, at first. I was a good student and I eventually made friends. I am not a troublemaker by nature and it was easy for me to follow the rules. I liked the school classes, reading and writing especially, but not many hours were spent there. The nuns taught us girls about cooking and sewing and of course, we were required to clean the school. We did laundry for the public as a way to partially fund the school, I guess. I was part of the choir and got to go to a few performances on the bus."

"How was that?"

"It was like we were caged birds on display. We had to look and walk and act precisely, like little robots. All of us girls had our hair cut into bob styles and we wore matching uniforms. Christmas was an interesting time there. Many of us stayed year-round and the nuns made Christmas a very special time. We still had religious studies, choir practice, chapel, and chores, but they played Christmas records, sang carols with us, and we each could use all the craft supplies we wanted to make gifts for each other."

"What were summers like?"

"We had school and chapel year-round. In the summer, though, in addition to our indoor chores we had work outside. I say had to, but actually I loved working in the gardens. Some of the students had to take care of the animals, but I got to plant and prune and harvest. That's probably why I love gardening so much now. One particular nun, Marcella, was really patient with me in the gardens. She was younger than the others and came from a farm nearby, so knew the soil and seasons like the back of her hand. She taught me what to plant together and which plants needed to be separated. She knew my favorite flowers and let me plant extras of those. I felt really special during my time with her. One day, when I was ten, she told me that I had been picked by Father Michael to help in the rectory. Once a week I was required to go help him organize his papers and tidy up. Before long that special time turned into a nightmare."

Loretta looked up at Brian, a blank expression on her face, and asked, "Are you sure you want to hear this?"

"Yes, Loretta. I think it's all part of your story and I want to know you. All of you."

"Father Michael eventually started treating me as his

marital wife. Of course, this was very confusing for me, and he warned me that if I ever told anyone about our secret ritual, God would strike my family dead. I still held out hope to be reunited with my family at that time, of course. Eventually, I became pregnant."

"You mean this went on for years and the nuns didn't know?"

"Oh, I'm sure the nuns knew," Loretta spat out with disgust. "I wasn't the first or the only one. I later learned about others with the same experience. Maybe you've seen news stories about the boarding schools and other horrible things that went on? I mean, sometimes a child would get really sick and then disappear. The doctor only came around every couple of months. That's what happened with me. Mother Cecille suspected I could be pregnant and called the doctor in to end the pregnancy. Sister Marcella secretly told me what was going to happen. She didn't tell me to run away, but I somehow got the idea from our conversation."

"You ran away?"

"Sure I did! I was scared of the doctor, and she said that a baby was growing inside me and the doctor was going to try to kill it before it could be born. She said it was very dangerous for me and she had heard of girls dying from it. I didn't really understand about abortion, but I knew I didn't want to die."

"What did you do?" Brian was in awe of this woman before him, who had overcome so much to become the incredible person she was.

Loretta described the escape and return to her grandmother's. "And then my grandmother convinced me that the best thing to do was to give the baby up for adoption. I was young - fourteen going on fifteen - displaced, confused, and desperate to belong somewhere."

"Loretta, you are such an over-comer. I would have had no idea that you had all that to go through. You seem so…well, put together and such a loving soul."

"Thanks, Brian. It was not easy. Not long after, I met Biggie. I thank God every day that it was Biggie that I met and not someone who was not good to me. In so many ways he saved me from what could have been a very difficult life. Our early years had some partying and some wild times, but when Pauline came along, we were committed to making a healthy family life, and I think we succeeded. As you can imagine, going back to any organized religion was hard for me, but at the time, we had an incredible pastor here, and it's only gotten better with Pastor Trevor coming on board. There was a safe opening for me to dip my toe back into the water and attend church only as much as I felt comfortable with. In the end, I learned that my faith, as it is now, not as I grew up with, is critical to my happiness. Biggie always had a strong faith, in an awe-shucks, down to earth way. He saw God in everything around him, and when Pauline was born, he treasured her as the greatest gift God could have brought us, and she is."

"I had no idea under his big persona that he was so faith-filled, but then, why would I? It's such a personal relationship, the one with God. While some people wear it on their sleeve, others live it in every breath. That sounds like how Biggie approached life."

"It's true. Once, Pauline got really ill and it was touch and go for a couple of days. Biggie was unwavering in his belief and carried us through it. When Pauline was pregnant with Lucy, it looked like there was a complication with the baby. It was then that I started getting curious about the baby I gave up for adoption. I knew it was a baby girl, but I hadn't learned anything more about her. I just thought…well, I thought it would be good to know if she had an illness, anything genetic that could also affect Lucy. As it turns out, Lucy is great, but I had already started this ball rolling trying to find my other daughter."

"Loretta, that's such a brave thing to do. Have you had any luck? I mean, I don't really understand how those things work, but it's a really big deal."

"As it turns out, I have learned that the only possibility of being in touch with her is for me to provide my contact information to the adoption agency, so I did that. Months went by and I didn't hear anything." Loretta walked to her desk and picked up a letter from a stack of papers and continued, "Then, the other day, I got this letter. I haven't told anyone yet about it."

"Oh, Loretta, is it from your daughter?"

"Yes. She's actually deployed. She's a linguist with the Army, but she cannot disclose her location. She was happy to have my contact information, of course has many questions, and wants to meet when she gets back to the States."

"How are you feeling about that?"

"It's amazing! I'm excited and anxious. I haven't told Pauline yet. I did tell her about the adoption and all that, but not that Beatrice - that's her name - had contacted me. I think she will be excited to meet her, but I'm not sure."

"I bet she will be. I mean, she's gaining a family member, not losing her mother's attention, right?"

"Of course. I think it makes a big difference that they are both adults with full lives in their own rights."

"Do you worry about how you will explain everything to Beatrice?"

"I do. I'll work with my counselor to find the best way to be honest, but not leave her feeling unwanted. I would never want to make her feel unloved. She did say that she was married. Her husband's in the army too, and they have a son. Isn't that something? I could say I have another grandchild, but it's not really so. I mean, I gave up all rights to claims on any of them when I signed those adoption papers."

"I guess that's probably true, but biology is still at play," Brian pondered. "Then of course there is the spiritual way to look at how we are all connected anyway."

"That's right. I never really thought about it that way."

A few minutes of pensive silence followed, as both sat deep in thought. Loretta finally spoke. "Oh Brian, I'm so sorry! I didn't mean to take us away from Dan and the whole Davies family and everything that came to light tonight. Let's talk about you and Dan, and what his condition means for the family."

LORETTA AND BRIAN talked for hours, speculating about how the ranch would be managed, which child, if any, would step forward and manage the ranch for Dan. They talked about the extended Davies family, the long history of perseverance they demonstrated, and Brian's move through addiction into recovery as a model of resilience for the whole family. With late night television droning in the background, they eventually fell asleep, Brian on the couch and Loretta in her recliner. It had been a long, drawn-out day filled with intense emotion.

15

———

*L*oretta startled awake in the early morning hours to the smell of fresh coffee. It had been a long time since she'd slept in her recliner. The chair had been a place of comfort in the early months after Biggie's passing.

"Good morning, sunshine!" Brian called from the kitchen.

"Good morning. Sorry, I obviously fell asleep. I hope we weren't in the middle of a conversation when I nodded off. That would be so rude."

Brian laughed. "No, we put the television on once we got too tired to talk and I'm sure we were both asleep in minutes. I think that was about three hours ago."

Loretta felt disoriented. "What time is it now?"

"About five," Brian responded as he handed her a fresh cup of coffee.

"We agreed to go to the eight o'clock service with the Davies, didn't we?"

"We sure did. We're to field questions and keep Dan

from getting tired out from too much conversation. I think they were planning to go in right at the beginning of the service and stay toward the back and then leave right before the end of the service."

"It's got to be exhausting for Dan to make an appearance like that. Even last night, which seems like weeks ago already, he seemed exhausted." Loretta felt oddly exhausted herself, but also relieved, anxious, and at peace. "I'm going to need a shower to sort myself out this morning. You're welcome to use the shower, too, if you want. Do you mind if I go first?"

"Go for it. Nothing like a good rinse to reset. I'm going to sit here in the quiet for a bit, if you don't mind. I may be out on the deck when you get out. Love me a colorful South Dakota sunrise."

"Enjoy. I'll see you in a bit."

Loretta emerged from the bathroom with coiffed hair, church clothes and a refreshed outlook. She joined Brian on the deck, coffee in hand. The colors of the sky were stunning. "What a beautiful morning!"

"It surely is. The sunrise is a thing of beauty this morning, with all the vivid colors against the clear blue sky. The thing about sunrises though is that they pass too fast. Some days I want to sit there and imagine I'm painting the sky with a big brush and watercolors, but it moves so much faster than I ever could. Not much of an artist here."

"I know exactly what you mean. It is a thing of

beauty to behold for sure." Loretta paused and took in the view before turning to Brian. "I think I'll make some eggs and toast. I feel like I should have some protein at least if I'm going to start in on the coffee like I do. What do you think? Would you like something?"

"Sure, sure. Let me come help you. I think the morning sky drama is almost over."

<hr>

"Would you please hand me..." Loretta turned to find Brian offering her the whisk she was going to ask for. Creating side by side in the kitchen with Brian was a breeze. "How do you do that?"

"We must just think alike in the kitchen. I mean, if it were me whippin' up those eggs, I'd be looking for a whisk or a fork and when I saw the whisk, I just knew that's what you'd want. I think it's kinda cool. You do it, too. I mean, didn't you just hand me a knife to put on the table with the peanut butter? I never asked for that."

"Ah, you're right. It is cool." Loretta poured the whipped eggs into the pan. "So, now what do you think I'm thinking?"

Brian sidled up next to Loretta, who was scrambling the eggs in the pan, and softly replied. "I think you're wondering how I have taken the story of your life that you shared with me last night, and if I'm ready to run away because it's just too much for me."

"You ARE good," Loretta admitted. "I hadn't gotten to the running away part yet, at least until after you eat these yummy eggs. But yes, I was wondering both how you're doing with Dan's diagnosis and with the load of my life I dumped on you…"

Brian put his arm around Loretta's shoulders.

"Loretta, I'm not a naïve man. I'm an old rancher who's been around and heard lots of things from people of all walks of life. What I heard last night was the harrowing tale of a young woman who weathered and overcame unimaginable things to become the God-loving, people-loving, kind, generous, bright, beautiful, and exciting person you are. I knew I loved you before, but somehow, and maybe it's just the process of being vulnerable with one another…" He planted a kiss on the top of her head. "…but I love you immeasurably now. You are just great."

Loretta rested her head against his shoulder, looking down at, but really not seeing, the scrambled eggs in the pan. After a few moments of staring, she shook her head to clear it. "Oh, no! Gotta get these eggs off the stove before they are burned to a crisp. Grab the toast before it burns too!"

With the pan in hand, she turned to watch him. "I have not met anyone like you, and with the wisdom of a lifetime of experience, I know you are one of the best, Brian. And if you eat these overcooked eggs, you'll be even better."

16

"*L*oretta, maybe you can answer this question." Beth summoned Loretta to the coffee ladies' table.

"What question is that?" Loretta was not a gossiper. This crowd knew that, leaving her to believe they only looked to her for something important and factual. Today she was distracted by her own issues.

"We heard about Dan's diagnosis and, of course, we haven't seen Yvette down here for coffee for weeks. We were just wondering how she's doing. She looked good in church yesterday, and she's a really strong woman. We just want to know, really, how we can best support her, and them?"

"That's really kind of you all. I think right now the best thing you can do is just reach out to her, send a message to let her know you're here for her and are willing to do whatever she needs. I know the church was talking about starting a food train for them, taking out food just once a week for now. We all know she loves to cook and it's a kind of therapy for her, so we don't want to take that away. But it might be nice if she had something she could stick in the freezer for later, when Dan needs more of her attention."

"We know you're close to the family and we appreciate your ideas. You keep us informed if there's anything else we can do, will ya?" Betty, a widow with a heart of gold, meant it when she said she wanted to help in any way she could.

"Of course, and you can always be in touch with the church office. Pastor Trevor is close with the family too and, while he can't share everything, he does have his finger on the pulse of where and when they may need help. They do have someone to help with the physical care when it's needed. It seems Dan's journey is at the beginning stages, and he still has more good days than bad ones, so they are not needing as much now as they surely will in the future."

"Thanks Loretta."

She addressed the table as she stood to leave. "You're welcome."

It really was not a good day for Loretta to be having coffee with the ladies, but she felt it necessary after the Davies' announcement. She was drowning in her own thoughts about Beatrice, Pauline, and Brian. She looked forward to a busy day at work, where she had a reprieve from perpetual strategizing the next steps in her head.

The workday moved along quickly. Loretta was folding sweatshirts and straightening souvenirs on the shelves when she felt a warm hand on her shoulder.

"Hello, beautiful. Can I take you away for lunch?"

Loretta smiled at the recognition of Brian's voice. She turned to face the ruggedly handsome cowboy. "Why hello there! I would love that. Let me just make sure Jessica is good with me stepping away."

———

BRIAN ESCORTED Loretta to his pickup, sitting in the alley behind the store.

"My chariot awaits you," he teased as he opened the door and invited Loretta to step up into the elevated truck.

"Why, thank you, kind sir," she playfully responded.

In a few minutes, they were at the city park. Brian reached into the backseat and brought out a cooler. "I know you only have a half-hour 'til you need to be back at work. I hope you don't mind a picnic lunch instead of a drive-through burger."

"I think it's a superb idea, actually."

"Let me come around and open the door. Hold on, just a second," Brian pleaded with the self-sufficient Loretta to allow him to treat her gentlemanly, like he was taught to do. He hurried around the truck with the cooler in one hand, opened the door and offered the other hand to assist with the high step down. They chatted easily as they walked toward a picnic table close by.

"You Davies men are so kind…and proper."

"Our parents insisted that we learn the social niceties they learned, like men walk on the street side of the sidewalk with the woman, whether it be a friend, a grandmother, a sister, or a wife, walking in safety between the man and the buildings. In fact, I'm sure my grandma would roll over in her grave if I didn't follow that rule."

"Those rules have little or no meaning to many of today's youth. I understand women are self-sufficient and all that, but honestly, for me, it's refreshing to have you show me those special kindnesses. I know you're doing it to enhance my life and not to put me down, as if I couldn't open my own door or walk safely on the sidewalk."

"Oh, for sure, that's how it's intended. You're clearly a capable woman, but I don't have that many opportunities to show you how much I care for you and that seems like a simple one, and one that comes naturally from my upbringing."

He continued talking as he pulled containers of fresh veggies and fruit from the cooler and opened them. "I hear what you say about young people seeing it differently. I don't know if they weren't taught or if they were chastised for practicing these gentlemanly acts, but I assure you my boys were taught and my daughter was taught to expect niceties, and she found someone who delivers them. And here we are - a chopped ham sandwich for you."

"Why thank you, kind sir! It's very nice of you to bring lunch." Loretta bit into the sandwich and followed with a drink from a water bottle. "Pauline and Chance are the same, but I'm wondering what it's like for Beatrice, who is living the military life. I would hope that she's able to retain whatever femininity she wants in that culture, but it's foreign to me."

"I think it's amazing now, how your life will be

enriched by learning more about her, and undoubtedly caring about her in a way you haven't been able to before. I sensed from her letter that she was excited to learn more about you and her biological family." Brian sat thoughtfully before continuing. "Is it okay to say that? Biological family? I don't mean to distinguish it that way, but I guess that's what it is."

"I struggle with it too. Maybe one day we'll just all be family, but for now, I am the birth mother and have no other context for a relationship with her. I'm not offended at all, and I do think you're right. I sensed an eagerness to become acquainted and for her to gain some history. Of course, I won't have answers to a lot of things she might be curious about, since I missed so many years with my own parents."

"Even that is part of her story, though, and one that will provide an opportunity for her to better understand how you came to the decision you did to release her to another family."

"I, of course, am eager to learn how she grew up and about her adoptive family. I have to assume it was so much better than I could have ever offered."

Brian placed his hands on Loretta's forearms and looked deeply into her eyes. "And in my humble opinion, so much better than the alternative that the school planned."

"Honestly, I haven't even thought about that. Obviously, I never saw that as an option, but you are absolutely right. I don't know if I could have lived with myself if they forced me to have an abortion. I mean that quite literally."

"I believe you do, and I'm grateful that didn't happen, and that scar was never yours to deal with." Brian offered Loretta fruit and veggies, which she waved away.

"You do make a mighty fine lunch, and I'm full. Now tell me, how are Yvette and Dan?"

"Had a great visit this morning. He was pretty tired after the weekend. No wonder - dealing with other people's reactions and going to church and all, on top of feeling sick. Got to spend a short time with Yvette while he had a nap. Then he wanted to chat about business and the ranch. He called Steve over, and the four of us talked through some of their ideas. I must say, those ideas are gosh darn good, and I'm thrilled that they thought to include me and want my input. I won't get into the details just yet. There's lots to figure out, but they've obviously thought about how they can manage everything and keep the business and property in the family. One thing about them, they are extremely fair. I mean, every child will have an equal share and an equal opportunity with them."

"It must be hard to see them thinking about those things the rest of us tend to push down the runway while just taking time to enjoy our grandchildren."

"Yes, but it's in their face, and they are managing it with such grace and dignity."

"Don't you think their strong faith helps them in that process? I mean, they each have a strong faith…"

Brian jumped in, "and a shared faith. I think it's one thing if each partner has faith and quite another if they both have a faith where they are living their collective lives toward one vision."

"I agree with you. Like with Biggie. We both knew, since we began our life together, that heaven was a goal we aspired to. There was never a doubt, so every decision we made together along the way considered how we could further that goal."

"The same was true for me and my wife. Can't imagine living any other way. I have friends where one spouse or the other has lost faith. In one case the husband vehemently turned away from the church. Sadly, they don't have a shared vision to guide their marriage anymore and it seems it's created a big hole in their relationship. Makes me sad for them. I see the wife at church often. At least she is able to hold on to and grow her faith."

"And maybe grow it in a way that would not have been as significant if she didn't have this challenge to face."

Brian nodded thoughtfully. "Never thought of that. You could be right."

"Thank you for that and thank you for this wonderful lunch. I know we're not sitting on the edge of the Badlands, looking out over God's country, but this is a beautiful reprieve from my usual lunch in the office at the back of the store, nuking leftovers or drinking stale coffee. Not to mention the delightful company you are. I appreciate you listening to me and helping me process this new development with Beatrice."

"And thank you for listening to me talk about Dan. Looks like we'll both be needing some talkin' and listenin' as this year goes on."

"Oh yes," Loretta agreed. "I feel so comfortable with

you and am grateful that we are both where we're at, in a place of openness, on the verge of new discoveries, and open to exploring what our friendship can be."

"Good thing we found each other when we did." Brian winked at her, the Davies' humor coming through. "And to think I found you in a snowbank."

17

Once they were back into their work routine, Brian and Loretta spoke daily on the phone. A week or so after their picnic lunch, Loretta was excited to share the latest news. "I did it. I talked to Pauline about Beatrice, then I reached out to Beatrice to see if she wanted a video chat since I have no idea when she'll be back in the States."

"That's fantastic! How did it go?" Brian had been driving the fence line, looking for breaches that needed fixing. When he saw that Loretta was calling, he pulled over and turned off the truck. His heart was warmed by her enthusiasm.

"We are going to have a video chat on Sunday after church. Pauline is really excited and hopeful that there will be another person that Lucy can eventually have in her life. I think the reality of Dan's illness and the fact that our generation is aging has caused her to really consider what extended family means."

"Sounds like Beatrice was interested in meeting too."

"She didn't hesitate. She didn't say it, but I'm guessing it won't exactly be a convenient time for her, but she offered no protest at all."

"So, tell me, does it feel exciting or scary, or both?"

"It is more exciting than scary. I think if I still had some feeling that this whole situation was sad and my fault, it would be frightening and I'm not sure I could follow through. But after therapy and really looking at how I got to this point, I mostly feel some ownership of creating an opportunity for healing. There's so much hurt in the world. If I can do this one little thing… although it's huge to me, it's small in the big universe of things… if I can do this one thing to bring healing, I feel really good about it."

The phone was silent, as both considered the magnitude of how Loretta's pursuit to find Beatrice had the potential to bring great healing. Loretta broke the silence first. "And you know what else?"

"Oh my, what more could there be? That is really a profound realization for you. What else?"

"I am so grateful to have you there holding my hand, virtually, if not in person."

"Oooooo. That's so sweet to hear. I'm glad you can feel my support across the space. I am in awe of what you're doing and honestly, I think it takes a really brave person to do what you're doing."

"Thank you, Brian. I do feel a bit proud of myself. Now tell me, what's going on for you?"

"I was just checking my fences and looking over

things. It's pretty dry again here and no rain in the forecast. The kids are all planning to come for a visit in a couple of weeks. It's the anniversary of their mother's passing and we like to spend it together, reminiscing and visiting her gravesite."

"What a nice tradition for you. I mean, I know it's hard, but it can also be a time of celebration."

"That's exactly how we see it. We cook some of the family favorites together. Haven't tried my Alfredo on them yet; we'll stick to the traditional. And we look at photos. This year I found some old video tapes that I sent off and made into a digital file that I can project. There's a movie of our family vacation to Yellowstone, one when we went to Fort Lauderdale and another of our road trip to Alaska. The kids were pretty young for all of these, and they haven't seen them, that I know of. It should be fun. I'll fix up a space outdoors and my daughter will bring a projector so we can watch it like we were at the old drive-in movies."

"That will be a great time. I think it's a super-neat idea."

"Actually, Yvette suggested it one day when I was talking to her. Seems we talk about every other day now, just checking in with each other."

"I haven't seen her around much. Do you think she would be amenable to a visitor?"

"I think so. You know, she can't really help Steve and Bella out at the dude ranch anymore. They bring Marco and Annie over to visit once in a while, but they're so busy, with Steve pitching in to help more. So I don't think she has as much socializing as she used to, and knowing Yvette, she really misses it.”

“She doesn’t have time for coffee, and I don’t see her around town anymore, so I thought maybe I would go to her.”

“Oh she would like that, especially if you have any juicy gossip to share since she’s missing out on the ladies’ coffee klatch.”

“You do know that I really dislike the gossip that goes on in that group. But I guess, for the sake of Yvette’s sanity, I’m sure I could find out something interesting to share so she’s not totally out of the loop.”

They laughed. As the laughter faded, Brian interjected, “You know, I sure do love you.”

Without hesitation, Loretta blurted, “I love you too, Brian.”

They sat in silence, soaking in the moment, until Brian asked, “You know what I’m doing now?”

“No, what?” Loretta responded.

“Smiling.”

Loretta found herself smiling too. “So am I,” she said softly. It felt good to feel loved and to share love.

“Well, hey, it’s so great to talk to you. I for sure can’t wait to hear about your video call on Sunday. I’m sure we’ll be talking before then. Is there anything I can do for you?”

“Keep me, and all of us, in your prayers, especially Pauline and Beatrice. You know, I didn’t really get to know my siblings and here, there is a chance to claim a relationship the girls didn’t know existed until now. As the mother, I’m hopeful that they connect.”

"I absolutely will keep you all in my prayers. I still think you're one of the bravest women I know."

"Thank you. I'm faithful, and there's where my strength comes from."

"Amen to that. Talk to you again soon. It's always so good to hear your voice."

Yvette was thrilled to have a visitor, and excited to catch up with Yvette.

"So, tell me what's going on with you and that handsome brother-in-law of mine. You two planning anything fun?" Yvette smiled, thinking perhaps the two might have some romantic escape planned.

"We both have lots going on right now and haven't gotten around to talking about what we might do when it slows down. For now, I'm content to have regular phone calls with him. I do have a bit of juicy news for you, though."

"Oh really? You know, I miss keeping up with the town gossip."

"That's what I thought, so I nosed around to see what I could learn that you might not already know. Here's one for you…" Loretta went on to share the debate amongst residents and landowners about the desire of a small group of investors to bring in a truck stop to the area.

"Oh, boy. I wouldn't want to be a homeowner near a

place like that, with all the truck traffic and such, but I certainly understand the desire to bring new industry to town. Doesn't seem like a place like that would be easy to staff, with the town already having to bring so many workers in during tourist season. That's a good one. What else you got?"

"What, that's not juicy enough for you? I thought that might provide at least three minutes of discussion fodder for you." The women giggled.

"You have to remember, I have been dubbed the queen of gossip in Buffalo Ridge, and now I have been dethroned by Lou Gehrig, himself."

"Ouch. The way you say that sounds awful and funny at the same time."

"Well, that's how it feels. Humor helps us through a lot. But you know I thrive on knowing what's up. Tell me another."

"Sure. You know that Basil boy, the one that flunked out of college and is the baby daddy to the Miles girl's twins? Well now he has another girl pregnant and her parents refuse to let them marry."

"What? Who is the girl and who are her parents?"

"She's a Martin from up north."

"There's no Martin girl old enough to see Emit Basil."

"I think that's the parent's point. She's only 15."

"O-M-G! Are they going to file charges?"

"Doesn't sound like it, so long as he agrees to leave the girl alone."

"Now that's juicy! Those poor parents, and that girl."

"I did hear she was a wild one, but that's why I hate

this gossip stuff. She could be a Sunday School teacher, as far as I know."

"I guarantee she's not. That's not a church-going family. The marriage has been rocky and they both drink. I heard tell that Social Services has visited their place a number of times. They have five kids and I think you're probably talking about their oldest, Savannah."

"Could be. I'm not familiar with the family, but I have included them in my prayers since I learned about it. It's such a life-changing experience for that girl. I think they should press charges, or that boy may never stop."

"It's just not the way it's done around here. Never know which neighbor you're going to have to rely on in the future. So the etiquette seems to be, make as few waves as possible."

"I know, but I can't always agree with that."

"I hear you. Now, what else? I'm sure you heard some other things, although that is a whopper right there."

"You are relentless!"

"I know. I'm also desperate. I'm not complaining. I will be here with Dan, of course, but I feel disconnected from the community we love so much."

"I know the coffee ladies want to come visit…"

Yvette shook her head and replied, "Yes, they do. But as the gossip girls, I don't want to be their source of a story. I mean, what we have going on here is private, to the degree we can have it be, and few trusted souls, like yourself, are welcome right now to take up our precious space. I know that may sound elitist, but I'm just trying to protect Dan's dignity and our privacy. There will be a time when it's different, but for now, that's where we're at."

"I totally understand. It was like that for Biggie and I when he was diagnosed with cancer. We tried to live as normally as possible for as long as possible, for us and for Pauline."

"Well, that's the other thing for us. I'm sure there's lots of speculation about what's going to happen to the ranch if Dan can't manage it. We're working our way through that, with the goal of keeping everything going as smoothly as possible and keeping it in the family. Brian's been helpful with that."

"I haven't heard much about that around town. I think everyone assumes that's private business and you both, because of the level of integrity you have, are held in high esteem and everyone wishes for the best outcome possible."

"I appreciate those kind words. It's great to know we aren't the main topic of conversation these days. That's a big reason why we tried to lay out the details in the beginning, so there wouldn't be a lot of talk. That won't stop all the speculation, but it seems to have helped."

"I do have a little more personal stuff to share. It might distract you for a minute, but it is really personal, and it can't leave our little circle here."

Yvette looked sincerely into Loretta's eyes. "I know I do like good gossip. But please, Loretta, know that I am fully capable of keeping confidences too. You know that."

"I do, Yvette, and that's why I'm going to share this with you. It affects Pauline, too, so there is some spillover to your family. Pauline and Chance share everything and

I know Chance is close to you and Dan." Loretta paused, drew in a deep breath to steady her nerves, and wiped moist hands on her jeans. "Pauline has a sister. A half-sister, really."

Yvette raised her eyebrows in surprise. "Really? Does she know this?"

"She does now. When there was that scare with Lucy, before she was born, I started investigating a baby I gave up for adoption when I was really young. I eventually told Pauline about it."

"Loretta, I had no idea. I'm sure there were circumstances that caused you to give the baby up. You're such a wonderful mother and grandmother." Yvette reached out to touch Loretta's clenched fist. "I'm so sorry for whatever you went through and the loss that it created."

With dry eyes, Loretta matter-of-factly responded to Yvette. "Thanks. It was a horrible thing that happened to me when I was away at Indian Boarding School, and I don't really want to rehash the details now. It's taken some painful doing, but I know now I did not do anything wrong to cause the pregnancy. When I found out that there was a plan to force me to have an abortion, I ran away from the school. My grandmother took me in and we worked with Catholic Social Services to find the baby a home. I was too young to raise her, and my parents were not in a position to be supportive."

"So, you know the baby was a girl."

"Well, when Pauline had that scare with the baby, before she was born, I reached out to the adoption agency to see if I could find out anything about the health of the baby I gave up. They told me she was a girl and the only way I could learn anything about her is if she wanted to contact me. I left my contact information with the agency and waited."

"Oh, Loretta, I wish I had known you were going through this. I would certainly have provided a shoulder for you."

"I know, and I appreciate you for that, but I really just had to do this by myself. Biggie knew about it, but I never talked to anyone else but my counselor about the whole ordeal. Anyway, Beatrice, that's the girl's name, contacted me recently. This Sunday we are going to video chat with her, Pauline and I."

"Oh, wow! That's amazing."

"It is, and I feel so honored that she wants to have that contact with us. She is somewhere in the world with the army and doesn't know when she'll be back in the States, but she has questions, of course, and I want to meet her."

"Are you nervous? I think I would be. But excited, too." Yvette refilled Loretta's glass with iced tea, then filled her own.

"I can't really say nervous. After a lot of therapy, I know that the pregnancy and giving the baby up for adoption were not the result of anything bad that I did. I was a victim of a horrible system, and my family was so dysfunctional at the time that they could not be there for us. It was the best decision possible, but I am very curious and look forward to explaining the circumstances to Beatrice. Unfortunately, I don't know much about my siblings or my parents since our family really fell apart. My grandmother gave me some information, but she bit her tongue a lot. I think that's where I get my avoidance of gossip from. She always said that gossip was the devil's work. I don't know that I believe that or would characterize it that way, but I do know that people can get carried away mischaracterizing things."

"I know exactly what your grandmother was saying. I don't think in terms of the devil that way, but it really can be a harmful practice, gossip. As much as I call myself the gossip queen, I do try to be factual and discerning about what I share."

"I believe that Yvette."

"How is Pauline doing with this? Neither she nor Chance have said a word to me about it."

"She's actually excited at the prospect of having a sister. She was a wonderful only child. She never acted spoiled, nor did she complain that she didn't have a sibling. But now, after seeing her father pass away, having a baby, and now Dan being sick, I believe she welcomes the idea of expanding her family."

"That makes total sense. She's such a loving soul I can't imagine she wouldn't be welcoming and excited. I have to admit, this is all a bit shocking. I mean, I would never have guessed. You've always just been so chill and never let on that anything like this ever happened to you."

"Remember, Yvette, I had Biggie to listen to me and protect me all those years. It wasn't that long after I had the baby that I met him, and we became a couple. I had to let him know about it. It was eating at me something fierce back then. He is the one that got me into therapy initially, and it was a good thing that he did. I really needed it."

"Who wouldn't? My goodness, what a lot for a young girl to go through. And, it confirms some of the ugly things we've been hearing about Indian Boarding Schools. It's worse than just forcing assimilation into the white culture, but totally taking the innocence of a child! Did you have any recourse against those running the school?"

"I imagine I could have, but for my own healing I chose not to pursue anything. I just really didn't want anything dragging on and making me revisit it over the years. It was just too painful to think about over and over again. My therapist was great and without her, I don't know what would have happened. Sadly, my grandmother, the one person I could reach out to for some level of support, passed away shortly after I left the reservation. She never made an excuse for my parents being so incompetent, but she did teach me a lot about how life had changed for her people, my people, over the generations and how the white influence caused a devastating loss of identity for Native Americans. Had I spent more of my youth on the reservation, I probably would have fallen into the same dysfunctional patterns and rebelled against the loss of the old ways, but that's unfamiliar to me since I was taken off the reservation."

"I can't imagine what it was like to have been taken away from your family so young."

"Nobody can. I lived it so I don't know anything different. I can see the pros and cons of it. You know that I have a strong faith. I'm not sure I could have developed that living with my mom. My dad left the home so he would not have been a shepherd to me. My grandmother was quite elderly and was always careful not to force her beliefs onto anyone. The boarding school had good and bad parts. Certainly, being raped was not something anyone ever expected would happen when they sent me there, and it didn't happen to all the children, just a select few. We did, however, learn a very different way of life than we would have learned on the reservation. But remember, not all of the children at the school were from the reservation. Some were from very poor families or were orphans."

"I guess I didn't realize that it wasn't only for Native American children."

"No, and because ours was the only school in the area, the kids who lived in town went to school with us, too. It was, for all practical purposes, just a regular school. But those of us who were boarders, we had chores and high expectations. We didn't have the freedom to play that the other children enjoyed."

"Oh, Loretta, won't you write a book some day and bring all this to light? It's fascinating and sad and an important lesson for our culture."

"I don't think I'll be writing about it. I've done a lot of healing and will do more with Beatrice and Pauline as time goes on, but I really don't want to dredge it all back up. There are others telling the story. I've read some newspaper articles about it, but I just don't want to go there. I have too many good things in my life right now, to go back through that."

"So, I just have to ask. Is Brian one of those good

things? I mean, he just lights up when he talks about you. I don't mean to pry, but if you want to share, I do hope that everything is great for you two."

"He has been a gift for me. He is so kind and caring. He knows about this and has been incredibly supportive and encouraging. I swear, that man could not deliver a judgment if he had to, he's just so…"

Yvette interrupted with a smile. "The Davies boys are a special breed. They want everyone to be great, happy, successful, and all that. It's one of the most endearing qualities of Dan and one of the reasons he has so much respect from others."

"I can see that. Brian is the same way. I am honored to know him and to be on his list of special people."

19

---

*L*oretta zipped up a warm winter jacket and pulled a stocking cap down over her ears. "I can't believe it's already time."

"It seems like just yesterday we had our first video chat with Beatrice. Now she's coming back to the States, and we get to greet her!" Pauline tightened the winter cap under Lucy's chin and covered her with a warm blanket.

"Too bad Chance couldn't join us," Loretta said as she opened the door. It was only late October, yet the South Dakota winter wind was blowing hard, creating a wind chill below zero.

"He sure wanted to come, but it's best that he keeps an eye on things and stays around for the repairman to fix our furnace." Pauline handed Lucy a stuffed toy, picked up the car seat and headed out toward Brian's warm pickup. "Poor Lucybug can't be sleeping in her snowsuit every night because the furnace isn't working."

"No, of course not." Loretta agreed. She kissed Brian

153

on the cheek as she climbed into the truck. "Thanks for taking us, Brian. I'm glad you were able to come along."

"Happy to be part of this celebration with you. Thanks for the invite." He watched, while Pauline settled Lucy into the car seat and got herself situated, before putting the truck in reverse.

FOR LORETTA, the fifty-mile drive to meet Beatrice seemed to take hours, yet only seconds, at the same time. "I don't know why I am nervous now. I mean, we have all met online and it seems to me we all get along well."

"Mom, I think it's understandable that you would be nervous. You want her to have a good impression of you, right? Well, we can let ourselves believe that can't happen virtually. Honestly, I'm anxious to see if there will be a big hug."

"Right?! I've been wondering the same thing. I think she will be cool, it's just my anxiety kicking in."

"So, if I could just butt in here a second," Brian interjected, looking first at Loretta on his right then in the rear-view mirror to Pauline. Seeing a nod from them both, he continued, "I'm sure it's going to be a great visit. As for the hug, who knows? That is not really predictable and may or may not happen spontaneously. From what you have both said, Beatrice seems like she has her stuff together. She said she grew up in a loving home, right?"

"She sure did, and I was relieved to hear that. I mean, what if she had not been better off than being with me? That would be crushing." Loretta had felt the weight of a brick house taken off her shoulders when Beatrice talked so joyfully about her adoptive family. She was the youngest child. Both of her adoptive parents had since passed, but she still was close with her siblings.

"Well, then, and I'm just speculating here, I think you are going to have a mind-blowing, earth-shattering reun…unification, I guess it would be. Have you thought any about what you want after this, assuming all goes as well as I think it will?"

"Like life with you, I want long walks talking in the Badlands, feeling the ancients there sharing their wisdom. I want family picnics and those horribly rigid, but necessary photo shoots to preserve us at our finest. I want laughter and love."

Brian gently brought Loretta's hand to his mouth and kissed it. "Then you, my love, shall have it all."

"Oh, get a room already, will ya?" Pauline teased and turned to Lucy. "Your grandma is like a giddy schoolgirl, ya know?"

Lucy giggled at her mother's silly talk. Brian and Loretta shared a smile held deep in their hearts.

SEVERAL HOURS LATER, they were back in the truck. Brian could barely contain himself. "Okay, you two. I believe I have just witnessed a genuine miracle. THAT was the most incredible display of genuine unconditional love EVER!"

He had been moved when invited to the meeting of Loretta and her adopted daughter, but now was even more moved by the meeting itself. The three relative strangers acted as if they had never missed a beat! Brian's eyes brimmed with tears several times during the three-hour coffee date. It was like their DNA, all three of them, was already familiar with one another's heart, melting a barrier that only the human mind could erect.

"Mom, your heart has got to be swollen with joy right now."

"Oh, it is Pauline! I feel like my prayers have been answered and this was divinely orchestrated. I mean, it's a maternal love story. My love for you was already huge, but it is magnified to see the grace you have shown as we walk through this new discovery and the magnificent expansion of our family."

"Oh, Mom, now you're going to make me cry."

"Cry on, girls, cry on!" Brian cheered. "Really, it is beyond love, what I saw. It's… well, it's a vision of the eternal love we all have, brought to earth for us to enjoy. What a gift!"

"Preach on, Brian." Loretta planted a gentle kiss on his cheek. She had never felt closer to any man, except maybe Biggie, but in a different way. She thought she knew love before, but the depth of feeling, the level of communication and sharing through expressions and posture, allowed her to feel so close to Brian that she felt a part of him, and he a part of her. This is the boundless love that she had heard others speak of, but had never truly experienced completely.

"Well ladies, where shall we go? I've had more than enough coffee for the time being. How about you?"

"I put venison stew in the slow cooker before I left the

ranch this morning. Would you two like to join us for dinner?"

Brian and Loretta looked at each other and smiled, knowing exactly what had crossed the others' mind. Brian spoke first. "I am absolutely open to that."

"Honey, it would be delightful to have dinner at your place. It's been a great day and I can't think of a better way to continue it." Loretta squeezed Brian's hand, eager to further this discussion at dinner.

BRIAN NAVIGATED the fresh-fallen snow skillfully as excited chatter filled the pickup cab. Lucy napped, lulled by the road noise. The thrill of the day carried into dinner. Chance was visibly excited for his wife and their growing family with the inclusion of Beatrice.

"Brian, did she take to you okay?" Chance had met Beatrice on one of the Skype calls and looked forward to the day they met in person.

"I think she did. She was interested in the ranch, having grown up on one herself, and seemed to ask all the right questions. I thought maybe she would be more reserved with me there, but not so. The three ladies rattled off questions right and left and answered just as easily. There was no hidden agenda or effort to be evasive that I picked up on. It really was an incredible sight to witness." Brian stood behind Loretta, one hand on her shoulder as he set a fresh glass of water beside her plate. "This woman here, she did a beautiful job filling in family history where she could, and she did it with such grace."

"Of course, she did. That's Loretta, and she passed that graceful action trait on to Pauline. Lucy is so blessed to have this pair as her mentors." Chance danced around the kitchen with Lucy before settling her into the highchair.

"Here we go, folks. Dinner is served."

"Honey, this is a beautiful meal. Thank you so much for having us over. How on earth did you have time to bake dinner rolls?"

"They came from the freezer, Mom. Yvette taught me that trick. 'Always have frozen dinner rolls on hand,' she said, 'it makes it look like you slaved away all day.'" Pauline winked at Chance. "I don't think your mom will care if I share one of her secrets with family."

"Your mom is certainly the hostess with the mostest, Chance. She is a woman I have looked up to the entire time I've known her." Loretta was sincere. As a meek newlywed moving to town with Biggie, she was impressed with the younger version of Yvette who seemed to have endless energy to give to church, family, and the community. She watched her for fashion and hairstyle trends, rarely daring to copy them, but gaining inspiration, nonetheless.

"That she is, but she sure has started to slow down since Dad got sick. She seems content to just be home with him, trying to make his life as good as possible."

"That would be your mom. I've been proud to call her my sister-in-law all these years they've been together. She was so good to me with your aunt Jerri Anne passed away." After a brief silence, Brian continued. "Are you all good if I offer up a blessing this evening?"

Heads nodded and Brian delivered a beautiful thanksgiving for the joys of the day.

PAULINE STOOD to clear the dishes. "I'm sorry I don't have dessert this evening, unless you want ice cream with chocolate syrup."

Both men jumped up and motioned for her to sit while they did the clearing.

"I don't need dessert, but I'm ready for more coffee."

"Mom, you're such an addict," Pauline scolded.

"I admit it. I'm helpless to fight off a fresh cup of coffee."

"Well, you might be in good company. I'll have a cup-o-joe, too." Brian was rinsing dishes and loading the dishwasher.

"You know I'm in. Hon, would you like a cup?" Chance opened the cabinet and retrieved the Folger's can.

"Nope. I'm going to clean Lucy up and put her pj's on. I'll meet you all in the living room in a few."

PAULINE NURSED Lucy to sleep while the others sipped coffee and chatted.

"I have to admit, we have ulterior motives to coming to dinner tonight." Brian started and Loretta continued, "We have something we want to ask you."

"Awe, Mom, you don't need to ask me if you can be

Brian's girl. It's nice of you to think of that, though." Pauline teased.

"Ha, funny girl you are. You have your father's sense of humor, I think."

"Could be, and you loved him, so I guess it's okay."

"True." Loretta took a long sip of steaming coffee. "No, it's sort of a business proposition, if you will."

Chance leaned toward the edge of his seat, entrepreneurial spirit guiding his attention.

Brian spoke first. "As you guys know, I have agreed to help Dan and Yvette run the ranch. Steve is busy with the dude ranch and greenhouse, Stella's staying in Arizona. Jesse is busy helping Kerry with her vet business. I know you guys are busy with the rodeo camps and running your own livestock, but we want to offer you the opportunity to join us."

Always cautious, Loretta interrupted. "Please know there's no pressure, but family business has some real positives as we look toward our retirement years and desire to leave a legacy. I'm not a wealthy woman, but I do have some inheritance from your dad, Pauline, and this is one way I, and Brian, can share with you."

"So what is this idea you have, and where?" Pauline rubbed Lucy's back as she lay asleep in her arms.

"Yvette and Dan offered me a little acreage for my help, and it just so happens that the land is adjacent to Steve and Bella's dude ranch. After much discussion and input from Dan and Yvette, we've decided to build an event center out there overlooking Sweetgrass Knoll," Brian announced.

"And we would love for you to be our partners if you are interested," Pauline offered.

"Wow!" Chance gasped. "Now back up a bit, here. So, Uncle Brian, what about your operation?"

"For now, Chad and Sam are going to take it over as the operators. Eventually all three of my kids will have a chance at the land, but I suspect Chad and Sam will buy them out and she will stop teaching. As for me…I think this old rancher's ready for something new."

"Those two ever gonna get hitched?" Chance couldn't resist ribbing his uncle whenever he had the chance. "I imagine they will. Who knows? Maybe they will be the first couple to christen this new event center."

Avoiding eye contact, Brian responded, "Could be." But he had other ideas.

"Just sitting here thinking about it, this is something I could get excited about," Pauline spoke cautiously. "With the baby and all, I'm around more and I love the thought of being involved with family. Of course, Chance and I will have to discuss it more."

"Sure, sure, take your time. We do have some design ideas in mind and want to break ground in the early spring with hopes of an August opening next year." Actually, Brian and Loretta had more than a few ideas and were ready to take them to an architect for development.

"Do you think that's doable?" Chance was skeptical. He had building projects on his ranch that never seemed to come in on time or at budget.

"I know it sounds idealistic Chance, but I do. I'm calling

in some favors. Already talked to some builders who could lead groups of laborers. There's plenty of folks looking to work and if we get a solid project plan in place and materials ordered, they have assured me it's reasonable." Brian had a good buddy from the AA program who was planning to retire his construction business. He agreed to manage this project as his last hoorah.

"That's cool. So, is there an investment you need from us up front?" Chance had plans to grow his own operation, but could reallocate resources, knowing it would slow down his own growth. He looked at Pauline. "Babe, I could totally see you being a big part of this venture."

"We were thinking of an investment of labor rather than money right now, with a future role in managing the bookings and coordinating events. You need to know that we have agreed, and I think you will too, to keep Dan and Yvette in the loop, and Steve and Bella, since it borders their properties, and they have an interest in the operation." Brian knew how important it would be to keep Dan involved and communicating as long as possible, and Yvette would need a future to focus on. A project like this to focus on, Brian thought, would relieve them of some of their daily stress, especially when they had no responsibility, either financially or practically, on the ranch.

Chance and Pauline saw Brian's motive immediately. "Sure, sure, that makes sense," Chance said.

"It's like having art therapy every day, or even occupational therapy where they could flex their creative and business muscles with no downside for them."

Pauline often thought in terms of the therapies she was involved with during her experience as a physical therapy assistant.

"We'll give it a good thinking overnight. Seems like there is nothing for us to lose but time, and a whole lot to gain, and I mean beyond potential income," Chance mused out loud. His business mind was rolling fast. "I think this community would support an event center. Mom and Dad could use the distraction; the location is an awesome one for events; and I can already imagine eye-candy photos for marketing in that area. We just need to think through how much time we, and I really mean Pauline, will have to devote to the project and operation, especially considering she is my right hand right now."

"Sure. Also think long-term. Maybe there are fewer hours available now, but more when Lucy gets older and goes to school. Brian and I are still very able-bodied and are committed to this joint venture. The other thing we can think about is bringing Trevor and Angela into the fold. They both have really good eyes for design."

"So, how joint will it be? You think you'll ever combine households?"

Brian laughed and Loretta blushed. "As you can imagine, we have talked about that, especially with me coming to the north side of the Badlands. When we have something solid to announce along those lines, we will certainly let you know."

"I am so happy we decided to go with the split loft and catwalk," Loretta called down to Brian, Pauline, and Angela below. Lucy chased a ball, toddling along as a one-year-old does. "It makes the best use of the clerestory windows, yet leaves the two-story height where it can be highlighted in the center. That grand chandelier you chose for the middle here is stunning, Pauline and Angela."

"I'm glad you think so. It really was Trevor's idea. He had seen one similar in Denver at a conference center there and he helped me find a really good deal on it. He's a great bargain hunter."

"Thank him again for us, will you, Angela? It's going to be a showstopper."

"Speaking of showstoppers, just how are your plans coming, Mom? The big day is this week!"

"Great, huh, Brian? They are coming along beautifully."

"That's right. Your mother has a knack for combining

beauty and simplicity in a stunning way. We're very excited to have this place ready, and we can't wait to christen it."

In August, as planned, the doors opened to 'The Prairie View', an extraordinary event center surrounded by the natural beauty of the colorful ancient heart of the Badlands. While the marketing materials varied, they all captured the beauty and history of the Badlands first, and secondly, the utility and uniqueness of the event center, situated near the dude ranch.

Brian and Loretta met just outside the doors, excited and ready to christen their creation, The Prairie View, with their nuptials.

"Brian, this feels a bit surreal. Everything is just so…"

"Perfect, like it was pre-destined?"

"Yes, all that, and more. We have all our children, grandchildren, your nieces and nephews…"

"Yours now, too. And Dan is having a great day. He and Yvette have really come to life in a different way, as much as this project has. I'm glad we decided to have them be our witnesses." Brian chuckled softly. "It would have been just overwhelming to have all our kids stand up or try to decide which ones should."

"I agree, honey. And Beatrice. Can you believe she went to the effort of getting leave to fly home and join us?"

"I can. She loves you, like she has always known you."

They stood in silence, holding hands, preparing to

walk in. "I know this project is done, Brian, but we are just beginning. Our future is going to be filled with exciting things. I have found it so easy to work alongside you…"

"And you as well. It's like we have the same rhythm, even our need for breaks and aloneness. It's taken a lot of years and experience, but I think we've learned to mimic nature with its energetic ebbs and flows and synchronicities."

"Well, whatever it is, it works. I'm thrilled to be standing here, at the threshold of our new business and our wedded life, waiting to open the door and be welcomed by our friends and family. I feel like we have arrived, after paddling through our own tortuous creeks, hitting sandbars and still waters, but always moving forward. Let's open that door and christen this place!"

ACKNOWLEDGMENTS

Thank you to Linda Zeppa of Intuitive Writing / Creativity, who enriches my writing life and soulful life with her knowledge, talent, skill, energy, and support. To the talented and proficient Angela of Angela Pruden Proofreading, thank you for your continuing support through excellent proofreading talent and encouragement. To those who have or do love me and those who refuse to, thank you for all the lessons! Finally, to my parents, siblings, children and grandchildren, and my special love, thanks for sharing life's journey—the good, the bad and everything in between. These are the stories that feed the imagination.

ABOUT THE AUTHOR

Kim Smart is a storyteller, nurse, attorney, PhD, and student of life. *Prairie Blossoms* is her ninth published novel and the sixth in the *Buffalo Ridge Ranch Series.* Kim's fiction works are inspired by personalities, experiences, and narratives from her life and the lives of friends and family. Kim has been a lifelong writer and today weaves in stories of the characters she meets at home and across the globe. Kim was raised in South Dakota, where *Prairie Blossoms* is set.

You can learn more at www.kimsmartauthor.com or through the social media links below.

Bella Giordano needed to find safety for her young son. On a whim, she moves them from Manhattan to the Badlands of South Dakota, hoping the small town life, away from mob threats and smog, will be good for them both.

Will grief dissolve and a new opportunity be enough to build a new family?

The second novel in Kim Smart's Buffalo Ridge Ranch series sets the table for new opportunities and the possibility of love. Will hurts heal and love grow?

TAKING CHANCES - BOOK - 3

Chance Davies, champion bull rider, goes from being rock star of the rodeo to broken and lost after a final ride turns into a tragic accident. He is forced to return to Buffalo Ridge Ranch for recuperation after many years on the circuit. Through hard work and challenging himself, his body starts to heal. But will he allow his mind and spirit to heal and open up to new opportunities?

Sheltered from love, Pauline Whyte was always a misfit in the small town of Buffalo Ridge where everyone knew her family's business. She escaped the town gossip for a few years by moving away, only to have to return to care for her ailing father. Somehow, in this small town, love finds its way to her. Can she accept it?

To let love in, they must overcome loss and pain. Will her misfit ways fit into his new life for a happily-ever-after?

The third novel in Kim Smart's Buffalo Ridge Ranch

series brings a story of overcoming the odds. Is that enough to find true love?

Dressing Up Stella - Book 4

Stella Davies lived far away from Buffalo Ridge Ranch. Fearing repeat abandonment, she built the life of a cowboy nurturing her herd on the rugged edge of nature in Arizona. But to find happiness, she must face these fears. When she moves to the remote high desert, she is forced to face her fears.

Ranching was in Brandon Cage's blood, but a new career as a lawyer changed his focus. He buried himself in his new profession and totally ignored his heart's desires.

Do they have the gumption to clear the way to give love a chance? Will their love arrive in time to find a life happily-ever-after?

The fourth novel in Kim Smart's Buffalo Ridge Ranch series is about overcoming past hurts and prioritizing love.

Grace and Grit - Book 5

Grace and Grit is a modern, heartfelt, clean, cowboy romance, that unites the rugged beauty of South Dakota's Badlands and ranch family life with the complexities of love, faith, and personal growth. The story introduces readers to Trevor, a young minister with a deep connection to the Buffalo Ridge community and his family ranch, and Angela, a dedicated emergency room nurse from the hustling streets of Manhattan. Their chance encounter in Buffalo Ridge sparks a romance that is both genuine and deeply moving. The emotional and spiritual connection between the two, and the personal crisis each faces, adds depth to their characters and their love story.

Let this tale of love's transformative power, set

against a stunning natural backdrop, be your journey today.

LYNX CREEK CHRONICLES SERIES

WHEN FIREWEED BLOOMS - BOOK 1

Anger, stubbornness, stupidity, fate or desire for adventure that led Jesse to the wilds of remote Alaska? The answer changes daily as she navigates a new chosen life in the wilds of remote Alaska, facing the harsh elements of virgin land in the shadow of Denali. Homesteading becomes a journey which opens an untamed river of intuition and feeds the garden of her soul.

Guided by the irreverence of unbridled nature, a wise grandmother, a faithful and flirty friend, and joined by a small, but growing community, Jesse wastes no effort to build a new life of solitude under the brilliance of the great northern lights.

STANDALONE NOVELS

TANGLED RIBBONS

The essences of individual humans are substantially more alike than they are different. Gertie Hall lives this truth as she rises from the young child of a Hitler's henchman to a world-renown advocate for human rights. Through scientific endeavors, humanitarian efforts and a tireless fight to right the wrongs of her father, she explores her feminine self, intellect, ingenuity, and grit.

A hole remains in her soul where two childhood friends were ripped away, and Gertie's own father was complicit in the disappearance of their families. *Tangled Ribbons*, scene by scene, captures the life of Gertie, intertwined with the stories of her friends, Sarah and Hannah, who flee fiery Berlin and establish new identities and new lives in far away places. Late in their lives, Gertie offers a heart-wrenching plea for amends and a new generation is enfolded in their healing.

Christmas Market reunion

Brooke Linton, 26, is stuck in a rut, aggressively pursuing professional recognition in corporate Miami with little time for fun. She tries to convince herself that life is great, so long as she has a good job, family at Christmas and she can sing in the church choir.

A chance meeting with an American in Amsterdam gives Brooke a glimpse into what life could be like outside the office.

After returning from vacation, her professional world falls apart. Through soul searching and discussion with a sister, Brooke grows to see this as an opening to create a life of her dreams. Little did she know how far those dreams would take her.

This sweet, wholesome romance will surprise and delight you with world travel, unexpected encounters, and fairytale weddings. The question remains. Can a chance encounter on foreign soil turn into something more? Get Christmas Market Reunion today and lose yourself in happily ever after.

www.ingramcontent.com/pod-product-compliance
Lightning Source LLC
Chambersburg PA
CBHW031752200726
48289CB00013B/796